I WAS JACK THE RIPPER

MICHAEL BRAY

Copyright © 2017 Michael Bray

The moral right of Michael Bray to be identified as the author of this work has been asserted in accordance with the Copyright, Designs and Patents Act, 1988. All rights reserved. No part of this publication may be reproduced or transmitted in any form or by any means, electronic or mechanical, including photocopy, recording or any information storage and retrieval system, without permission in writing from the publisher.

Imprint: Megalodon Press

MICHAEL BRAY

DISCLAIMER FROM THE AUTHOR

Before we dive into this story I thought it was a good idea to say a brief word or two to make sure we are all on the same page. This book, although based on the awful Whitechapel murders in London in 1888, is NOT intended as a historically accurate novel. That said, I have put a lot of research into this book to make sure it is accurate to the time frame, however, if you are coming here looking for a theory on who I think Jack the Ripper was, you may have come to the wrong place. For all of the speculation on who may be responsible in reality from Tumblety to Sir William Gull and everyone in between, I have decided to meld fiction into fact, and so my Jack is not a person who existed in reality and as a result not one of the existing suspects.

This was done so I could make the very best work of fiction that I could. There are plenty of historical books that deal with who may or may not have been the killer, this is not one of those. This is very much a fictional story created around some of the most brutal crimes ever to take place in England. If you came in expecting something else, then you may want to stop reading now and move on and get something from the true crimes section.

If you are still with me and want to come along, then I invite you all to join me in nineteenth-century England, a time when it was dark, cruel and brutal, and we are about to pick up the story of a writer who is about to be visited by a man with a strange and spectacular story to tell….

MICHAEL BRAY

CHAPTER ONE

Whitechapel District
London, England 1907

The man kept his eyes fixed on the ground as he turned onto Union Street, head lowered against the chilly December winds which were bitter with the threat of snow. The homes here were clean and tidy, the streets free of the urchins and scum who frequented the slums which were less than a mile to his back. Even these homes paled in comparison to the ornate stonework and brass door knockers of Westminster, however, his journey would not go so far as that. It was here, in the middle classes that was to be his ultimate destination. Twice since he set out that evening he had considered turning back, and yet the fire that burned within him had compelled him to continue the journey. He turned left, making his way to Mountford Street and noticed another change in his surroundings. Here the homes were larger, two-floor affairs, set aside in twin rows on either side of the streets. His eyes darted from door to door, window to window and once again he considered abandoning the entire journey and returning to his lodgings. He slowed the pace of his brisk walk to better see the numbers of the buildings, searching for the one given to him in the letter he received.

The man came to a halt a third of the way down the street, taking a moment to pull his coat closer against the chill bite of the wind and sleet which blasted his face with each gust. He regarded the building. It's unremarkable facade was of grey stone, and the windows were dark and featureless, save one on the lower floor, which was alive with the orange glow of firelight. A short pathway led to three stone steps, and the door, its lion head knocker swaying under the assault of the wind. It was as unwelcoming as it was impressive. The man glanced at the small brass plaque mounted beside the door, verifying that he was in the right place, the name etched on it wet with beads of rain

HAPGOOD.

He heard a sound coming from further down the street and watched as a young couple approached, arms linked as they whispered to each other. They looked into each other's eyes as they passed, reminding him of long forgotten terrors and pain which brought a chill to his heart to rival that of the bitter wind. As the couple passed, he lowered his head and turned away so that his features were unseen, an old habit that had not faded with time.

The couple continued on their way, not noticing the man as he stood before the house. He watched them as they continued their slow walk oblivious of the conditions until they were out of sight around the corner. Burying those long repressed memories that tried to bubble to the surface, the man smoothed his hands down the front of his topcoat, brushing away the light dusting that was beginning to form as the sleet transformed into snow. The man took out his pocket watch. His host was expecting him at nine sharp, and as a man who prided himself on punctuality, he intended to wait until the hour struck, storm or no storm. He looked in the direction that the long gone lovers had gone on to wherever they were heading and wondered if they were out to see a play at the theatre, or heading home to spend the evening together in the warm and away from the worsening conditions. A bitterness welled up within him, which he pushed away. He knew if he didn't, it would feed the demon which lived within. Age had brought patience and some control of that beast, but the advancing years had also brought with it questions about his own mortality. He was no longer a young man who was fit and strong. It seemed to him that in a short space of time he had changed into something else, an old, withered thing that he hardly recognised. He checked his watch again, and waited for the minute hand to strike the hour, then climbed the steps and knocked on the door. A light filled the glass arch above the door, which in turn was opened to reveal his host for the evening.

CHAPTER TWO

Charles Hapgood was a slim man, dressed in a casual unbuttoned white shirt and brown trousers. His long nose, sloped shoulders and low brow gave him a bird-like appearance.

'Mr. Hapgood, I presume?' the man said, holding out his hand to the host.

'Yes, please come in,' Hapgood said, showing his guest into the hall before closing the door against the shriek of the wind.

'Please take off your coat, sir, the weather is ghastly this evening.' Said Hapgood, gesturing to the coat stand by the door.   The man complied, removing his topcoat and hat, and placing them on the stand, and then turning back to Hapgood who gestured to the roaring fire in the study

'Please, come and warm yourself by the fire Mr....' Hapgood trailed off, waiting for the visitor to introduce himself.

'Miller,' replied the visitor as he made his way into the study. His eyes scanned the room as he approached the large fireplace, above which was a painting depicting the resurrection of Christ. One wall of the study was filled with books stacked from floor to ceiling with all manner of volumes on every possible subject. Beside the two chairs set out by the fire, sat Hapgood's desk, which was just as chaotic as his book collection.

'Would you care for a drink Mr Miller?' Hapgood asked as he poured himself a large brandy.

Miller nodded as he warmed his hands, rubbing them together to restore feeling. Hapgood returned with the drinks and set Millers on the small table between the two chairs, the golden liquid warping and reflecting the firelight. His own he retained, taking a thoughtful sip as he observed his visitor.

'Please take a seat,' said Hapgood, gesturing to one of the high-backed chairs as he sat in the other. Miller sat, folding his thin hands in his lap.

Hapgood studied his guest, soaking in the details and trying to make sense of the strange series of events which had led to their meeting. Miller was tall and very thin with high cheekbones which dominated his face. He would appear ordinary if not for his eyes, which were a brilliant shade of blue. The rest of the man was unremarkable, Hapgood would even go so far as to say anonymous. His mouth was a thin pursed line above the chin, and he wore his hair parted to the side, which Hapgood noted was greying with age. He had what Hapgood called the timeless appearance, making estimating how old he was impossible.

'So, Mr Miller,' said Hapgood as he took another sip of his drink. 'May I inquire as to the exact nature of your request to see me this evening? My office tells me you were quite insistent and that it has something to do with my work.'

Miller gave no reply. He stared at the flames, lost in his thoughts.

'Please, Sir, It is irregular for me to meet prospective clients in my home. If you prefer we can arrange a meeting to discuss this in my office through the correct channels in due course.'

He was about to speak again when the Miller looked at him, causing Hapgood to draw breath. The colour of Miller's eyes was even more mesmerising when they were fixed upon him. They were unnaturally blue as if lit from within. Hapgood felt that rather than at him, it was as if Miller was looking *through* him and was privy to all of Hapgood's innermost secrets. The entire incident lasted just seconds before Miller pointed to a stack of brown files on the small table beside Hapgood's chair.

'I understand that you are writing a book on the Whitechapel murders of eighteen eighty-eight.'

'Yes, that is correct. Am I to understand you have information on the case which might be of benefit to my research?'

'I understand Inspector Abberline himself is assisting in your research,' Miller said, a small ghost of a smile forming as he said the inspector's name.

'Yes, Mr Abberline was gracious enough to offer his assistance, however, I fail to see the relevance of...'

'And how much have you written of this book Mr Hapgood?' Miller asked, turning his icy gaze on him again.

'I fail to see why that is of any relevance. Please, Mr Miller, state your business or I'm afraid I will be forced to ask you to leave. I have much work to do.'

The near smile faded, and Miller leaned back in his chair and sipped his brandy. 'My intention is not to offend your gracious hospitality, in fact, it is quite the opposite. I am here to give you the greatest of all gifts.'

'I'm afraid I don't understand.'

'My understanding is that you are regarded as one of the finest writers in London. In fact, upon my inquiries as to who might be best suited to my needs, it was your name which on almost every occasion was recommended to me as the man with whom I should speak.'

'Thank you, Mr Miller, I am pleased my ever gracious peers regard my work with such esteem.'

Miller took another sip of his brandy, enjoying the warmth radiate through his body. 'I wish for you to write my memoirs. Age is becoming a burden to me and life is starting to take that which for so long I took for granted. You will, of course, be paid well for your efforts, even more so than in simple financial terms when the details of my life story emerge.'

With a frown, Hapgood set his glass on the table. 'My apologies Mr Miller, I'm afraid that you have wasted your time. I am, as you are aware, incredibly busy with work on my book, and would be unable to find time to do as you request. Besides which sir, I am afraid that I do not write autobiographical material. My field is more in historical fact than memoirs. I can, however, recommend several of my colleagues who would be happy to...'

'No,' Miller said, setting his empty glass on the table.

Hapgood saw a slight shift in his guest's demeanour, a barely perceptible flash of something within those eyes which was gone as soon as it appeared.

'Mr. Miller, I'm sorry but I cannot help you. There are many skilled and qualified biographers in the city who would be happy write your memoirs for you.' Hapgood said, standing and motioning towards the door.

Miller did not stand. He looked Hapgood in the eye. There was something there, something Hapgood was struggling to identify. Arrogance perhaps, or anger. It made him both curious and afraid.

'Mr. Hapgood, please sit.'

It was not a request. There was an air of authority in Miller's voice which until that point had been absent. Hapgood was starting to think there was more to his guest than he first thought. He sat, and the two men stared at each other to the backdrop of the crackling heat of the fire.

'I'm afraid that your colleagues, fine writers as I'm sure they are, just will not do under these circumstances. I need the best, and that, good sir, is you as we have already established. Now please, allow me to explain before you reject my proposal.'

He waited for a protest, and when none came, he went on.

'I'm dying, Mr Hapgood. Even as you and I converse, I feel the spectre of death's presence. My body is becoming old, my bones tired. I fear it will not be long before this world and I part, and I welcome it. This world and I have spent far too long in each other's company. Before that happens, there is much to be told which needs to be committed to official record before it is lost forever.'

Hapgood drained his brandy and set the empty glass on the table.

'I'm sorry to hear of your troubles Mr Miller, truly I am, but as I have stated, sir, I am unable to offer my assistance at this time. I am far too busy.'

'You don't understand Mr Hapgood, there is a great burden upon these shoulders which I cannot take with me to the grave. You must hear what I have to say.'

'I am no priest, simply a humble writer. Perhaps the church will hear your confession.' Hapgood was growing frustrated, yet curiosity kept him from ordering his guest to leave.

Miller spoke slowly, the transformation from the mumbling man who first entered the house startling in its rapidity. 'I need no confession, for I have committed no sin. My imminent death bears no consequence to my visit to you this evening. I am more than prepared to stand before God and justify all that has passed. I chose you for a reason, and I swear it, one way or another you will hear what I have to say before this night is done.'

Hapgood struggled to formulate a response. He was excited and angry, afraid and curious. The mixture of emotions made any rational thought difficult. 'Mr. Miller, I meant no offence.' He stuttered. 'However, I am simply trying to avoid wasting both of our respective time. I am behind schedule on my work, and if I am to finish then I am afraid it must have my full attention.'

Miller leaned forward, staring into Hapgood's eyes as he spoke in a near whisper. 'Mr. Hapgood, I don't think you understand. What I have to tell you will render your current work obsolete, I'm afraid.'

'That is a matter of opinion, and frankly, Sir illustrates a lack of respect. You enter my home under irregular circumstances only to then disrespect my profession. I'm sorry, Mr Miller, that won't do. I am afraid I will have to insist you leave immediately. I am unable to help you.'

'Those files,' Miller said, ignoring Hapgood. 'Am I correct in the assumption that some of those are inspector Abberline's personal notes? His own private thoughts on the Whitechapel case?'

Hapgood nodded 'Yes they are. The inspector and I are close friends, and since his retirement, He is assisting me with my research. I fail to see why this is at all relevant.'

'And, Mr Hapgood am I correct in my

assumption that within those notes there is information that only the inspector would be privy to? In other words, information never released to the public during the initial investigation?'

'Yes, Inspector Abberline's personal thoughts on the case are in my files, however, I fail to see how any of this is pertinent to our conversation.'

'It's pertinent because it will enable me to explain to you why I am here. I trust you are familiar with the case and its finer details?'

Hapgood was growing angry and could feel his cheeks flushing. 'Yes, I pride myself on my research. My exploration of the case is at an advanced state, as I have stated.'

'Would you be so kind as to retrieve Inspector Abberline's files? In particular, the murder which took place in Hanbury Street.'

'I am familiar with the case.' Hapgood snapped. He wanted this man out of his house but was curious as to where the conversation was heading.

'Forgive me, my intention is not to question your methods, nor your ability. Remember, I come to you today because you are the best. Please, Sir, if you would be so kind as to indulge me and do as I ask, then all will become clear.'

'And again I remind you I am familiar with the case. Please, delay no further. Either state your business or leave me to mine.'

Miller stared at Hapgood then reached into his breast pocket and placed two brass rings on the table between them. Hapgood picked them up, turning them over in his hands. They were small and stained green with age. He noted that they were of low quality and in poor condition. Not something he would expect a man of Miller's stature to carry with him.

Hapgood set them back on the table. 'I'm not sure I understand.'

'Please Mr Hapgood if you would please check the files for the Hanbury Street murder, then everything will become clear.'

Hapgood went to his desk, leafing through the papers and folders until he found the one he was looking for.

'Do you mind if I smoke?' Miller asked.

'Please, go ahead,' Hapgood said, for the moment distracted by his search. Miller took an ornate wooden pipe from his pocket and began to stuff it with tobacco as Hapgood continued to leaf through the documents.

'Mr. Miller, I see nothing in these files that relate to these rings,' Hapgood said, watching Miller for his reaction. Miller spoke around the pipe which hung from his lip as he ignited it.

'Perhaps the good Inspector's personal notes will reveal more than the public reports. May I suggest you review those instead?'

Hapgood opened a second folder which contained the personal journals on the case sent to him by Abberline. Hapgood had not yet read any of the contents, his current progress in his book was based on the facts of the case, and the Inspector's insight was still an area which he had not explored. He began to leaf through the various notes and papers, some of which were copies of documents Hapgood had already seen, but with handwritten notes and thoughts of the inspector included

'Apologies Mr Miller, but again, I see nothing that would...'

Hapgood stopped speaking and drew breath. His gaze drifted from file to Miller, then to the innocuous brass rings which sat on the table, and finally back to Miller who was staring into the flames of the fire as he smoked his pipe.

If Hapgood had not chosen that moment to return his gaze to the file, he would have seen the small smile cross Miller's lips as he exhaled a plume of grey smoke.

'They took a while to remove, Mr Hapgood,' Miller said, his voice taking on that icy, sinister tone again. 'I almost gave up but they eventually slid free. The fat whore didn't deserve such trinkets.'

Hapgood looked again at the words penned in black ink on the copy of the autopsy report of Annie Chapman, the victim of the Hanbury Street murder.

The victim is missing two brass rings, which appear to have been removed by the murderer himself as a keepsake or memento of his violation of this poor woman. I have informed Godley that this information is not to be released to the public at my express instructions as it may aid us when we catch the devil who committed this vile act. If only he and I know of this detail, any suspect we apprehend and can have confess to this knowledge can only aid our investigation.

Hapgood felt a surge of anxiety as he looked at the unremarkable man seated by his fire, in his very own home. He tried to speak but could muster no words, his brain struggling to accept the possibility of who sat before him.

'I trust now I have your full attention?' Miller said, taking another long draft on his pipe.

Hapgood wanted to run, yet a combination of his instinct as a writer, his thirst for knowledge and the complete and total fear which now controlled his entire being kept him from doing so. 'How did you, how could you know... '

Miller looked at Hapgood and smiled around his pipe. 'I believe we both know the answer to that particular question. Go ahead and say it, Mr Hapgood. You will feel better for getting it out in the open.'

Hapgood struggled to formulate words. His brain was filled with static as the enormity of the situation became clear. 'You are him, aren't you? You're the Ripper.'

Miller smiled and smoked his pipe. 'Mr. Hapgood, you look quite unwell. Please sit down.' Miller said, gesturing to the chair opposite.

On shaky legs, and in something of a daze, Hapgood did as instructed.

'Mr. Hapgood, you look like a man who could use a stiff drink. May I?' Miller asked as he gestured towards the drinks cabinet. Without awaiting a response from his dazed host, he stood and poured them both a large brandy, before returning and setting the glasses on the table. Miller sat, and for a time, there was silence except for the hiss and crackle of the fire.

'Is your intention to kill me?' Hapgood said, unable to think of anything else to say.

Miller laughed, a hearty booming sound which echoed through the empty house and had no place after such a revelation.

'Of course not, Mr Hapgood. A talent such as yours deserves its place in the world. I simply require your skills to tell my story. Rest assured, you are in no danger.'

'But you *are* him. The Whitechapel Ripper.'

Miller inhaled on his pipe and blew a cloud of smoke. 'Yes. I do believe I was.'

Hapgood nodded, and with a shaky hand picked up and drained his brandy glass. 'What do you want from me?' he asked as the burning liquid radiated through his body.

'I want you to write, Mr Hapgood. To do what you do best. I will tell you all that there is to tell, and you will document this to the very best of your ability.'

Hapgood looked at Miller and almost screamed outright. He somehow stifled it, instead releasing just a sour, brandy flavoured belch. Miller's blue eyes shone with their intense brilliance, however, the flames of the roaring fire now danced within those eyes, reminding Hapgood that he was in the company of the devil himself. Roused from his daze by the bitterness of the brandy, He managed to compose himself enough to speak to the monster which sat before him.

'I know of the terrible deeds you were responsible for, and yet I'm curious as to why you think I can help you? Why would you come forth now? The story of your deeds are well known. There is nothing more I can tell.'

'We have already discussed my reasons. I will not explain again.'

Hapgood managed to still the cyclone of thoughts in his brain enough to regain some control. 'Why me? Why choose me over anyone else?'

'Because you are the best. I have done my research. I know all there is to know about you.'

'Forgive me if I disagree, sir, for I lead a private life and am not one to boast to my peers. Perhaps the word you received of my ability was incorrect, particularly in regards to such a…unique story.'

Miller nodded. 'Nevertheless, I still know of you.'

'Perhaps someone else will hear your story and-'

'You are Charles Michael Hapgood, aged thirty and born in Liverpool, before moving to London three years ago. You are married to Jane Hapgood, aged twenty-three, and have a daughter aged four. She would of course ordinarily be here, but instead, she is visiting your mother in Liverpool, who is sick with pneumonia. She is due back here next Tuesday.'

Hapgood was stunned. Miller seemed so ordinary, that it was hard to associate him with the vile and horrible things he knew this man had done. He knew the sensible option would be to have no part of it, to go to the police, but the writer in him wanted to know. He could not rid his mind of the details he knew from his research. The five vicious murders, the mutilations, which, if he were to be believed, had been committed by the beast sitting across for him.

Miller spoke, Snapping Hapgood back to the

present.

'I can see that you are interested in hearing my story, and why would you not be? Think about it, Hapgood. You will become known as the man who will tell the story of the Whitechapel murders from the man who was responsible. A unique opportunity to cement a legacy for you and your family and a place in history as one of the greatest writers who ever lived. However, if we are to do this, then we do it now, this very evening.'

'You wish to start now? I'm not ready I need to prepare I...'

'It must be told now by the light of this fire or not at all. This is the only conversation you and I will ever have. Now please, get something with which to write, as there is much to tell.'

Hapgood was still in a daze as scrambled around the room to his desk, tossing his stationary aside until he found a stack of new paper, ignoring the screaming instincts to run. He could not afford to waste such an opportunity, even if it put his own safety at risk. He moved everything off his desk into a pile on the floor set the paper in front of him and refilled his inkwell before selecting a brand new pen with which to write. He looked at Miller sitting by the fire, then screamed at himself that this wasn't Miller. That was likely not even his real name. He was sitting across the room from Jack the Ripper.

Miller watched his flustered host prepare his desk to begin writing then stood. 'May I suggest another brandy before we begin? I suspect that you may need another taste to ensure your mind is clear.' Miller said, curling the corner of his mouth into a humourless smile.

Although Hapgood could feel the alcohol beginning to work on him and under normal circumstances would never drink whilst writing, he felt that another glass could do no harm. He nodded to Miller who poured them both a fresh drink then returned to his seat by the fire.

'I am ready,' said Hapgood, unsure if that was true. He didn't think it was possible to ever be ready for something like this, something so unique. He was still in shock, his mind full of conflict and questions. With a trembling hand, he dipped his pen into the inkwell and waited.

Miller took a deep breath and stared into the fire for a full minute before he began to speak.

'There is much that has happened to me during my lifetime. History will remember me as a monster, a lunatic. My life's work consumed me for many years before it began, and to this day still sits at the forefront of my mind, even if I am far too old and sick to act upon it. The physical form is a strange thing, Hapgood. Frail and weak. Filled with limitations. I wonder if my life would have transpired in a different fashion had certain events not taken place during key periods of my lifetime.'

'Something triggered you to begin your...work?' Hapgood said as he started to write in the hope that doing something familiar would help him to cope with the situation.

'Yes. The man who I became was not the man that was born. I have known love, Mr Hapgood, and I have known loss. I have known cruelty, and I have seen the monster that lives in every man walking the earth. I have also known fury. Vengeance. Retribution. Of course, even in the telling, I'm not sure if you can understand, however, tell it I shall and I shall endeavour to ensure you see the world as I saw it. There is much I have forgotten over the years. Memory fades with age. However, I remember with absolute clarity the day that my journey to my work in Whitechapel began. In fact, the details are as clear as if it happened this very morning. It is complete in every detail. I was just a boy then of course, but if we are to explore the origin of the man I would become, this is where we should begin. I'm sure you know by now that Miller is not my birth name. For the purpose of this story, I shall choose one that is equally false. Miller was the name of the place I finished my work in London as you know it and so Miller I shall be.'

'Of course. The Mary Kelly Murder took place at Miller's Court.' Hapgood muttered, sickened by the casual way his visitor had named himself after his most brutal of murders

'For the purpose of this story, as I am aware you

will need a name for me, you can call me Edward. Edward Miller, a boy, a child who after one singular event in his life found his path forever altered. Are you ready to hear it, Hapgood?'

Hapgood glanced up at Miller then looked back at his paper. He was still terrified, but the shaking had subsided and the brandy had helped him to regain a little control. 'Begin when you are ready, Mr Miller.'

Miller closed his eyes to gather his thoughts, rolling back the years, 'It was a cool day in September when my journey would begin. The wind was in my hair and my heart raced with the healthy feeling of exertion. It was a sense of freedom which can only be appreciated as a child without worries or concerns. This is how it happened, Mr Hapgood. This is where my story begins.'

CHAPTER THREE

He ran, arms and legs pumping with the furious and tireless energy that only children can muster. He rounded the corner at full speed, weaving between the myriad of torsos and legs of the giants around him who were busy about their business at Spitalfields Market

'Edward… wait for me!' came the breathless voice behind him. Edward paid no attention, instead ducking under a trader laden with bottles, and almost crashing into a stall housing fruit and vegetables

'You watch yourself, lad,' bellowed the red-faced trader, but Edward paid no mind to the man, nor the burning in his legs or the pounding of his heart in his chest.

'Wait for me, please,' whined the breathless voice from behind for the second time.

Edward brushed a sweaty lock of hair behind his ear and skidded to a halt by the imposing wall of the London docks. His senses filled with the fresh, salty scent of the sea and the symphony of noise and activity. He sat on the ground with a thump as his pursuer jogged to a halt beside him.

'Bleedin' hell Eddie, you nearly took that old fella off his feet back there.'

Edward said nothing as his friend sat beside him. The pair looked out in silence for a while at the slate grey waters and rolling clouds as cargo of all shapes and sizes were loaded and unloaded by their respective crews.

'Mr. Jones will have us if he finds out we didn't go to school today,' George said as he wiped his arm across his sweaty brow.

Edward looked at his friend with his cool blue eyes and smiled 'You sound like you're scared of old Jonesy. Come on George, nobody will miss us.'

George sat on the dock wall, swinging his feet

against the stone as he looked into the water and considered what to do. 'What now then Eddie? It looks like rain.' George said, squinting into the sky.

Edward followed his gaze to the thick thunderheads that rolled towards them. Some were a deep purple, scattered like bruises over the ocean. Edward thought for a moment and then turned to George.

'There's a freak show in town. I hear they have a two-headed boy and man no bigger than your hand.' Edward said as George looked at his palm and wrinkled his nose.

'Impossible. Nobody is that small.'

'We'll just have to see, won't we? Come on.'

'How will we get in without money?' George said.

Edward considered the question as he watched seagulls circle over the dockyard.

'I know where my mother keeps some money at home. My father will be at work and my mother helps at the orphanage. Come on, we'll get some money then go see for ourselves.'

'Aww come on, let's just go back to school before we get into trouble.' whined George as Edward stood and stretched.

'Are you really scared of everything George? All you do is complain.' Edward said with a shake of his head as he started to walk back the way they had come.

'It's alright for you, my father is a cruel one, last time I pulled somethin' like this he gave me a caning.'

'You should learn to talk your way out of it Georgie. Lucky for me mine are always busy.'

'You sure your Father won't be home?'

'He works as a foreman at one of the warehouses near Bucks Row. He's an important man. There will be nobody at home.' Edward said as they moved deeper into the Whitechapel district. The walls were close and wound over and under each other in a confusing maze of arches and alleyways, but he knew them well. He liked it there, getting lost and exploring. Everywhere people bustled, Edward finding comfort in the sheer volume of excited chatter which surrounded him.

'Edward, I don't like it here. My dad says nobody who lives here is up to anything good.'

'Edward turned, stopping dead and looking George in the eye. 'I live here, George.'

'Oh... I... I didn't mean you, I meant...other people,' said George, lowering his gaze and watching his feet as they kicked at the cobbles.

'Come on George, let's go get that money!' Edward said, grinning and clapping his friend on the shoulder.

They made their way past Christ Church, the large gothic building chiming to signal midday as they crossed into Fournier Street, the overcrowded houses jammed together in tight rows. They moved passed the brewery on the corner of Heneage Street, then onto Chicksan Street, where more red brick homes were crammed together. Some of these one-room homes had up to twenty inhabitants, and as George looked at the filthy children who sat outside open doorways, their eyes devoid of hope for any kind of respectable life, he wished he had just stayed in school. Edward and George reached the corner of Duke Street and stopped.

'This is where I live. Come on, let's go in through the back.' Edward said.

The back street was narrow and cobbled with barely enough space between the back to back houses. The two boys started down the street when Edward pulled George out of sight and ducked behind a wall.

'What is it, Edward?' whispered George.

'My father. He should be at work, not at home.' Edward said as he peered around the corner.

His father stood by the wood gate which led into the rear yard of the house. Several other men milled around in the alleyway chatting in small groups or standing around idle and smoking, making small talk with each other.

'What's going on?' George asked, trying to peek around his friend.

'Shh,' Edward replied, pushing his friend out of sight and returning his gaze to the alley. As he watched, the gate opened, and a man who Edward had never seen before came out of the yard. He clapped Edwards's father on the shoulder and the two shared a few words before the man laughed, and headed up the street away from the crowd and out of sight. As soon as he was gone, another of the waiting men spoke to Edwards's father, who then opened the gate and allowed the man to enter. Edward ducked back around the corner and leaned against the wall.

'What is it Edward, what's happening?' George asked.

'Not sure. Looks like men from my Father's work.'

'What are they doing at your house?'

Edward didn't answer. Instead, he headed back towards Duke Street and the front of the houses, which were gloomy and in disrepair. A few doors stood open, curious and tired looking ghosts of people stood, some smoking, other chatting in groups of two or three in the absence of anything else to do.

The door to Edwards home was faded and

swollen with age. The windows were filthy, and instead of curtains, there was a grubby linen sheet pinned to the inside of the frame. Edward walked to the door, and touched the handle, before turning back towards George.

'Wait here, I'll get the money,' he said, before inching open the door, and slipping inside.

The room was dark, the overcast daylight struggling to breach the heavy sheet over the single window. Edward took a moment to let his eyes adjust to the gloom, watching as specks of dust swirled in the air. He moved quietly and was nimble as he skirted around the edge of the room towards the kitchen where he knew the money was kept, but instead froze and held his breath, his young brain trying to register what he was seeing.

At first, he thought she was being attacked and was about to yell out when he realised that his mother was encouraging the man who was on top of her.

'Go on, that's it,' she said as the man writhed and grunted. Edward was frozen, unable to comprehend what he was seeing. The naked man's hips moved back and forth in a furious piston-like motion. 'You like that don't you love?' he panted in her ear as he groped at her pendulous breasts.

'Come on then, let's be avin' ya,' she said, willing him on.

Edward crept closer, ducking into the shadowy recess of the corner between the old bookcase and the wall, affording him an uninterrupted view of the horrific scene in front of him. He felt sick, but could not take his eyes from the tangle of flesh which writhed and twisted on the floor of the kitchen. He thought of the group of men outside, and how one by one Edward's father was letting them into the house. He now knew why and what these men were doing. Worse, he knew his father not only knew but was allowing it to happen.

A sudden flush of anger welled up within Edward as he watched the man who was still thrusting with great enthusiasm on his mother grow increasingly noisy.

'Nnh, I'm close now love. Are you ready for

this? Here it comes,' he panted at her, his hands now gripping her shoulders as he increased the ferocity of his motion.

Edward could not move, his feet rooted to the spot. His vision of their family unit, of a father who worked as a foreman and was an important man and his mother the homemaker who would tend to them both was shattered. Although they lived in a poor area they had always been a step above desperation, or so it seemed. He watched as the man let out a great moan, and froze, clenching his hairy buttocks together, before flopping down on Edward's mother, breath wheezing, and rasping.

'Fuckin' lovely that was my love. Just what the doctor ordered,'

Edward watched as his mother took a cloth and wiped herself. The edges of her thighs were rubbed red. 'All part of the service, love. You be sure to come again,' she said with a cackle which startled Edward. This was not the mother he knew, the caring woman who would be in the kitchen preparing food or cleaning when he came home from school. This woman was a stranger.

The man stood and picked up his trousers from the floor, and pulled them on, then adjusted his shirt. 'Worth every penny that was love. You've got a lovely cunt.' He said to her as he pulled on his cap.

'And a big fella like you deserves somewhere warm to put it. Now do me a favour and tell him to send in the next one will ya, love?' She asked, now propped up on her elbows.

'Will do, poppet. I'll see you next week,' The man said before putting a few pennies in the jar beside the sink, the one Edward had come home to get money from for the freakshow. The man straightened his clothes, opened the back door and slipped outside, closing it behind him.

Edward waited in the shadows, still hidden from view. His face felt hot and tears stung his eyes. He wanted to ask his mother why she would do such a thing. Before he could do anything, someone else opened the door, a large, flabby man who Edward recognised. He worked as a butcher at the docks.

Mr McGuffey. Edward's mother smiled as he entered, unconscious of her naked body where she lay on the floor, legs open and ready to receive her next customer.

'Ello love, what have we here then?' she said, looking Mcguffrey up and down. He was already sweating, as he unfastened his trousers and took them off, revealing his flaccid and tiny penis.

'Mr. McGuffey has some meat for that hole of yours,' he sneered at her, licking his plump lips.

'Come on then butcher man, let's be avin' ya,' she said, beckoning him to her.

Edward watched in horror. It was worse than the first. The man sweated and grunted at her, calling her things which Edward had never heard before. His tears were now dry on his cheeks, replaced with a revulsion and sheer disgust at this creature he used to refer to as his mother, the mechanics of the whole ordeal making him feel nauseous. He could bear no more and slipped away back the way he had come. He was grateful for the fresh air that greeted him. He inhaled in great gasps and the horrors he had just witnessed replayed themselves over and over in his mind.

'Did you get the money?' George asked, oblivious to what had just transpired.

Edward said nothing, instead walking past George and heading down the cobbled street towards the dock area.

'Eddie?' George said, trotting to keep up 'Are we going or not?'

Edward wiped his eyes and turned to George.

'Go back to school, George. Just leave me alone.'

'But you said we were going to the-'

'I've changed my mind. Just go, leave me alone.'

'Eddie come on, this was your idea,' George shouted after him. 'Eddie!'

Edward didn't turn around and soon became lost in the crowd. George stood for a few seconds, contemplating how much trouble he was going to get into, then started on the long walk to school, preparing for the caning he knew was to come.

Edward walked in silence, hands in pockets and head down against the steady rainfall. He was cold but did not care. His mind still was filled with the images of the horrific things he had witnessed. He wept, the rain masking his tears as he moved amid the scores of people on the overcrowded, stinking streets. The rain intensified and an ominous rumble of thunder sounded somewhere in the distance. Edward wasn't sure where he was, he knew he was somewhere close to the London hospital, he could see the spires of its three towers in the distance. Soaked to the bone, he ducked into a side alley. Rotten food and waste were piled high against the walls, making him gag. He moved deeper into the alley and ducked into a recessed doorway and sat down on legs which were still shaking, resting his back against the filthy brickwork. It offered him some protection from the elements, and more importantly, solitude to try and process what he had witnessed. The tears came again, great sobs of frustration and anger that felt as if they would have no end. The storm was now close, the rain no longer falling but being driven into the streets with overwhelming ferocity and mingling the putrid stenches together into a disgusting soup. As he sat amongst the filth, an inquisitive Rat, large and black scurried alongside him and began to rummage amid a pile of rotten fruit oblivious to Edward and his troubles as it sniffed at the stinking black mound. Edward stopped crying and watched the Rat as it explored the waste, pausing occasionally to stand on its haunches and sniff the air. It looked at Edward with its black, lifeless eyes, whiskers twitching as the two stared at each other. Deciding that Edward was no threat the Rat returned to the rubbish and started to eat a slab of rancid meat. Edward watched, mesmerised by the way the Rat's sides moved as it breathed, the way it nibbled at the decaying flesh. He leaned close, reaching towards the animal, which was unaware as it continued to eat. He lunged at it, grabbing it around the neck. The Rat squealed and squirmed trying to claw at Edward, who despite almost losing it managed to retain his grip around the creature's neck. The Rat was still squealing, a sound which Edward did not like. It reminded him of the noise the butcher, McGuffey was making when he was on top of his mother. Overcome by a wave of frustration and anger Edward squeezed the rat's neck, feeling the soft tissues compress under his grip. The Rat's movements began to slow, its legs kicking. Edward held it close, looking into its black eyes as he increased the pressure. There was a wet crunch, and the Rat went limp in his hands. His heart raced with excitement, and there was a strange sensation in his groin, something which was new to him, but not unpleasant. He turned the dead animal over in his hands, running his fingers over its wet fur, feeling the ridges of its bones, the softness of its skin. He was aware of what he had done, that it was considered wrong and yet felt nothing. No emotion, no sadness, no sorrow. He felt as cold and empty as the rat's dead stare. He turned the rat over onto its back, gripping with both hands and running his thumbs down its underside, before stopping at the flabby stomach. He pushed his thumbs into the flesh, tearing the skin until it gave way, thick gloopy innards squirting out and over his hands. Still, he felt nothing, and continued to pull, tearing the rat's stomach open. He looked at the blood on his hands, then at the hole where the rat's stomach once was. He smiled, pushing at the wet entrails with his index finger, assessing the texture, the way everything was put together. It was still warm as he dug his fingers in and scooped out the contents. He rubbed them between thumb and forefinger, squeezed them in his fist. He dipped his index finger into the cavity of the rat's stomach, and wrote his name on the wall, then lined the individual letters of his name with the entrails which were sticky enough to hold in place on the soot covered brick as he completed his macabre work. He held the empty carcass up to his face, and put his nose close to the stomach cavity, inhaling deeply. The copper and filth smell did not repulse him. It felt good. It felt right. He touched the cavity of the stomach, probing, wishing he had savoured it more, taken his time. Already he wanted to do it again. He looked at his name, smeared on the wall in blood and entrails and grinned. He could do it again. Would do it again. It made him feel good and would be his secret, just as his mother and father had theirs.

Hapgood stopped writing and looked at Miller.

'That was where it began? With a rat in an alleyway?' he asked, setting down the pen and stretching his fingers.

Miller shrugged his shoulders. 'Yes, it appears so.'

'Discovering your mother in such a way…I cannot begin to imagine how such a thing would feel.'

'I was just a boy. Children should not be subject to such shocking imagery.'

Not just children Hapgood thought as the crime

scene photographs of Mary Kelly danced into his mind. 'What happened after the Rat? He asked as he picked up his pen.

'For a while, nothing. I continued to live within the lie created by my mother and father and indulging in my own new found hobby at the same time. Often I would stay away from school and sneak into the house to watch the perversions taking place before heading out to do more of my own, fuelled by the things I saw. I was cruel to those animals, Hapgood. I took retribution on them for the things my mother and father were doing. Three months passed and I had added three more rats, a cat and two dogs in the pursuit of my new hobby. My father, who had lost his employ at the docks for drunkenness had found his moods becoming increasingly black, and combined with his addiction to alcohol had become unpredictable. It was this inherent mean streak, this bitterness which next manifested itself in spectacular fashion. You ask if it was the rat which started my own dark path, and in a sense, it was, but not as much as my father and my whore mother. They were the true creators, they were the ones who shaped who I was to become. If there is blame to attribute then it is to them.'

'What happened?'

'Like the rest, I can recall it with almost perfect clarity, complete and it every detail. It was an evening late in December. My mother and I were sitting down to eat when my father arrived home drunk and angry which had become his habit. I wonder if perhaps his increased need for alcohol was his own way of dealing with the horrors of the actions of his wife. If there ever were a pivotal moment for what was to come later, Mr Hapgood, this was it. A course of action was about to be forged that would be the guiding light towards the thing I would later become.'

CHAPTER FOUR

He arrived, stumbling as he fell through the door.

Edward and his mother looked up from the kitchen where they sat at the table, the stew his mother had prepared still steaming in the pan. Edward looked at his father, his shirt filthy and untucked, his face dark with stubble. He was a large, broad-shouldered man, with a soft stomach brought on by his drinking.

'What the fuck are you two staring at?' he grunted as he sat at the head of the table and glared at them both, his eyes bright and hateful. Edward had seen this before and knew the slightest provocation would result in a violent attack.

'What's wrong with you two cunts, then?' he said, chuckling to himself as he took a great ladle of the stew, and slurped at it, not bothering with a bowl.

He winced, spilling some of the hot liquid down his front and on the table top. 'Too fuckin hot you stupid bitch!' he roared, tossing the ladle on the table.

'I'm sorry James, I didn't realise I...'

He leaned across the table and punched her in the face, knocking her off her chair to the ground. Edward sat and stared, unsure what to do as his father looked at him

'You keep that fuckin' hole of yours shut lad, or you'll get the same.' He said as he staggered to his feet, knocking his chair over. Edward's mother lay on the floor, a great welt appearing under her eye, her nose and mouth bleeding.

'You stupid, stupid cunt, Iris. You burned my mouth with this fuckin' slop. Fuckin' look at it,' he said, gesturing to the pot of stew.' I wouldn't feed pigs with that shit.'

He looked at Edward for approval, saw none, then turned back to look at his wife where she sat on the floor. 'Let's see if you like it hot, Iris, let's just see,' he said, as he picked up the pan of stew and poured it on her. She screamed and writhed on the floor as Edwards father looked on laughing.

'Not nice is it, Iris,' He bellowed. 'You don't seem to be enjoying it. I told you I wouldn't even feed pigs with it.'

'Leave her alone,' Edward screamed. 'I'll tell the police about what you do here.'

'What did you say you little bastard?' he said as he staggered towards Edward who was trying to keep some distance from his father by backing away around the table.

'I'll tell,' said Edward, his cheeks flushing with anger. 'I know about the things you make mother do.'

Edwards's father tossed the table aside and lunged for his son. Edward turned to run, but stumbled over his own feet and tumbled to the ground.

'You little cunt!' He said as he pulled Edward to his feet by his shirt. 'Make her?' he said through clenched teeth. 'I do what I have to. To bring fuckin' money in so you and her can live under my roof instead of the streets. Look at her.'

He dragged Edward over to where she lay, the skin of her face and hands pink and blistered from the stew.

'What other use is the stupid fat fuck?' he spat at Edward as he hit him hard in the face, sending him crashing into the sideboard, then onto the floor next to his mother. The pain was explosive, taking his breath away and causing him to see white flashes when he blinked.

'I'll teach you, boy. A father and son lesson, how about that?' he said as he dragged her by the leg towards the centre of the kitchen floor, before tearing off her skirts and exposing her naked lower half. He turned to Edward, pulling him off the floor to his feet, and holding his face inches from his own.

'I know you know how to boy because I have seen those stained sheets of yours,' He said as he tossed Edward on his mother. 'Now fuck her.' He barked.

'James, don't do this I'm sorry, I didn't mean for

it to be so hot,' Iris moaned through her broken face.

'You shut that fuckin' mouth of yours, cunt!' James screamed, before picking up a knife from the side of the sink, and showing it to his son. 'You better start to fuck right now or I swear to God I'll cut her fuckin' throat then yours.'

Edward looked into his father's eyes and knew beyond doubt he intended to do it.

'Father, please, don't make me do this,' Edward sobbed.

'Father?' he sneered. 'I'm not your father you little bastard. We don't know who your father is. He could have been any one of the men that have been on top of that fat bitch in the last ten years.'

Edward turned to his mother, who was looking at him through puffy eyes. 'Just do as he says Eddie, it will be ok...I love you no matter what,' she sobbed holding his hands.

Edward closed his eyes and tried to think of something, anything but what he was about to do.

It was his hobby that helped him through it.

Thinking of ripping and tearing them apart, figuring out how they worked inside. After it was done, Mother and Son lay on the floor, one crying in pain from her injuries, the other blank and devoid of any emotion, the man of the house standing above them, a wide grin on his face.

'See how easy it is, Boy? You and that bitch deserve each other, I'm leaving,' he slurred, as he tossed the knife on the floor.

Edward's mother pushed her sobbing son away and climbed to her feet.

'James, please, don't leave us.' she sobbed, following him to the door.

'You and that little bastard can fend for yourselves now Iris, I'm done with you both.'

'Please, James don't leave us.' she was begging, clinging to his shirt sleeve as he opened the door. 'I'll get rid of him, I never wanted him either. He's a parasite, please, just stay, we can get rid of him then it will be just the two of us. Please,'

He turned and raised his fist, causing her to let go and shy away from him. He glared at her as

Edward watched from the kitchen floor, still naked and on his side, his knees pulled up to his chest as the words of his mother cut him deeper than he could have ever imagined.

'See how you cunts do without me to put food on the table,' he said, then slammed the door, plunging the house into silence.

Iris stared at the door as if doing so would will her husband to come back. When it became obvious it wasn't going to happen, she turned towards Edward, who was still on the floor.

'This is your fault,' she screamed, spitting blood. 'If you hadn't said anything about... about the things we do....' she trailed off, sobbing.

He closed his eyes and wept. His mother walked towards him, and for a moment, he thought it was to hold him or bring him comfort. Instead, she stared at him where he lay.

'I would swap him for you if I could. I don't want you, I never did. He drinks because of you. Because he has to bring up another man's child. No wonder he left. You did this. You broke up our family.'

She walked past him, leaving him cold and broken on the floor. He heard her go upstairs and close the bedroom door. Edward didn't move. He lay where he was and stared at the knife his father had dropped. Despite everything, all he could think of was how it would feel in his hands, and how easy it would be to cut things up with it rather than using his bare hands. Eventually, he got to his feet and started to clean the mess from the kitchen. The knife he kept.

CHAPTER FIVE

Hapgood sat silent, pen hovering over the paper. He watched Miller, who was staring at the wall, his thoughts elsewhere. Despite all that this man had done, evil deeds for which there could be no forgiveness, Hapgood found himself feeling sympathy. He couldn't comprehend the kind of damage such a traumatic experience would do to a child.

'I'm sorry for your ordeal, Mr Miller. Nobody should have to experience the things you speak of.'

Miller didn't answer. He stared at the fire, a deep frown etched on his face.

'Have you ever tried to find out what happened to your father?'

'To what end? He was dead to me from that day. The irony is that for all of my hatred, in the eyes of the public, I have become that which I hated about him. I truly am my father's son.'

Hapgood nodded, still struggling to handle how surreal the situation was.

'As I'm sure you are aware, my work in Whitechapel bore no signs of sexual coupling. This was not a coincidence. After the events of that day when my childhood was snatched from me, I would never again be able to achieve sexual arousal of any kind through natural methods.'

'Then why do it? Why brutalise those women in such a way?'

Miller pondered, his index finger tapping on the arm of the chair as he composed his thoughts. 'For a time, my mother and I continued our lives. Of course, our relationship was irreparably broken and we barely held conversation. She blamed all that had happened on me and I was so embarrassed that I declined to argue. I grew up isolated and alone, is it any surprise I found solace in violence?'

'This is beyond violence.'

Miller smiled, staring off into the fire again. 'I

spent my young life hating that woman. I longed for her death, then when it came I wept because it occurred to me that I was now truly alone. Even at the end as she lay on her death bed she wouldn't look me in the eye. Such a fragile creature I was then, Mr Hapgood that I sobbed and begged for forgiveness for something I was innocent of.'

Silence filled the room as Hapgood finished writing and took out a fresh piece of paper. 'What happened after your mother passed?'

'I was fortunate to find employment at the Royal London Hospital, cleaning the operating rooms and moving the dead to the morgue. I used to watch the surgeons as they worked on their patients, how they made their incisions, how the organs were removed from the body. It's surprising how much one can pick up if one watches. I enjoyed my employ there surrounded by the spectre of death. Its constant presence provided the comfort I had sought for so many years. I believe I was the only one in that place who prayed for the wounded to die rather than be saved. Even so, I wasn't entirely alone in the world. My childhood friend, George also found employment at the hospital. He and I were friends as children until his mother married into wealth following the passing of his father. As a result, our lives would move on to very different paths. Where I was a mere porter, George was studying to be a doctor and had the financial backing of his mother and stepfather to do it. Even though our lives had taken those different paths the two of us had remained close.'

'That must have brought you comfort.'

Miller shrugged. 'Not particularly. I yearned for something to fill the emptiness which had grown within me, something to give me a sense of normality or belonging and I was envious of George as he climbed up the social ladder. Even then I felt fractured as if I were two people inhabiting one body. I wanted a normal life and yet there was a darkness I was curious to feed.' He sighed and folded his hands. 'You may ask why I choose to spend so much time dwelling on this period of my life when there are other areas of it I'm sure you would prefer to discuss. To that, I say all in good time. This next part of my life of which you will hear was instrumental in shaping what was to come later, and it is important I tell it so understanding may come about what took place later. As with all things that melt a man's heart, a woman was at its centre and this story is no different. Allow me to tell you of true love, Mr Hapgood and how dangerous that emotion can be. I was wavering on the edge of the precipice between sanity and madness. Little did I know that she who I imagined would be my saviour would become the catalyst for all that was yet to come.

CHAPTER SIX

The walls of the operating theatre reverberated with the screams of the man who lay on the wooden table. Two nurses restrained his arms as the surgeon worked at the gaping stomach wound.

'Nurse, More Morphine for this man. He is wide awake.' Bellowed the doctor as he tried to keep a bloody grip on the man's stomach.

'I'm sorry sir,' she said as she administered a large dose to the man, who still writhed and bucked in agony, his eyes bugging out of his skull.

'This man is a mess.' The doctor muttered to himself as he tried to close the wound.

'He was stabbed sir,' said one of the nurses as she struggled to hold the man down.

'I can't see a thing.' Grunted the doctor. 'Miller, clean up some of this mess and don't get in my way!'

Edward moved around the doctor with practised ease, wiping the blood from the table and the body. His eyes were wide as he watched the doctor work. Edward could see inside the man's stomach, the fatty yellow inner flesh visible above a great train of intestine. He longed to see more, and as he cleaned he wondered what other secrets lay within that hole.

The patient gave one last spasm and then lay still on the table. The doctor continued to work on the wound then paused to listen to the man's chest.

'This man is dead.' He said, wiping his bloody hands on his apron.

Edward barely heard him. He was looking at the man's eyes and had seen the life fade from them.

'You will get used to sights like this boy,' the doctor said, mistaking Edward's wonder for fear. 'Now take this man to the morgue, and clean up the rest of this mess.' Edward nodded and watched the doctor leave, the nurses following him.

The room fell silent. Edward approached the body on the table and looked into the stomach cavity. He wanted to touch it, to experience the feel of those slick, cooling innards on his skin. He reached out, heart thundering at the idea. As his hand drifted closer to the wound, the door to the operating room opened and the doctor returned. Edward withdrew his hand and did his best to remain calm. 'Leave that for now boy. The patient's daughter is here for news of her father, and I have more work to do. Go outside and inform her of his death. The family name is Simmonds. Go now.'

Edward was about to object that such things were not part of his job, but the doctor had gone, leaving Edward and the corpse alone. Realising how close he had come to being caught and how he couldn't afford to lose his job, he decided the best thing to do would be to distance himself from temptation and do what had been asked of him. He skirted around the body, giving it a last longing look, then exited the operating room.

He made his way through the gloomy halls, the

moans of the injured and dying no more than background noise as he twisted his way through the throng of people who were lingering in and around the hospital. The sick were everywhere and some had been there since he had begun work earlier that morning, still waiting to be seen by a doctor. It was too crowded, too hot, and with the memories of the gaping stomach wound still fresh he needed to clear his mind before informing the patient's daughter of her father's demise.

Edward made his exit and stood on the street, taking huge gulps of soot tasting air. Lost in his thoughts, he didn't notice the woman approach until she lay a hand on his shoulder.

'Pardon me, sir,' she said.

The girl was slim, her blonde hair in curls that stopped on her shoulders. Her skin was milky white, her eyes brown.

'I didn't mean to startle you. I was hoping for news of my father. He was attacked by a gang and stabbed.'

'What is your father's name?' Edward mumbled,

staring at his feet.

'Simmonds. Derek Simmonds. My name is Lucy. I'm his daughter.'

He forced himself to meet her gaze. 'I'm sorry to inform you that your father is dead.'

She nodded, then forced a smile. 'I do not know what I am to do now. I expected this with how bad his injuries were. Even so, I hoped he would be saved.'

'I'm sorry. There was nothing that could be done.'

She looked away down the crowded street, lips pursed together as she fought not to cry. 'Thank you for trying to save him. I appreciate the work you doctors do.'

'I'm afraid I am no doctor, Miss Simmonds. I am far from such a lofty stature.'

'Doctor or not, I think everyone who works here to try and help people and save lives deserve praise. You are good people.'

'There is nothing much good about me, Miss. Nothing at all,' he said, again staring at the ground.

'That I don't believe. My father always says – *said*, that I've always had a good understanding of people and I believe you to be a kind man, even if you do appear troubled.'

He couldn't believe the strength she was showing. Somehow, despite the terrible news, she was holding steady. 'If you would come with me into the hospital, I will give you your father's things.'

'I'm afraid to follow you into there Mr....'

'Miller. Edward Miller.'

'Edward. I like that name. Edward, I'm afraid to follow you back into that place as I fear I will not be strong enough. Does that sound idiotic to you?'

Miller shook his head. 'Not at all. In truth, Miss, I believe grief is the most normal reaction you could have at a time like this.'

Despite everything, she managed a smile. 'You have the strange ability to ease my sadness, Edward. Of course, I know this battle is one I will soon enough lose, but I appreciate your kindness.'

'I've done nothing, Miss.'

'Will you please call me Lucy? There is little need to be so formal.'

'Lucy. I say again I have done nothing but bring you the terrible news I was asked to deliver.'

'May I ask something of you?'

Edward nodded, still unable to make eye contact.

'Will you wait with me when I go back in there? I fear I cannot face this alone.'

'Of course. I will wait for as long as you require.'

She sighed and glanced at the imposing building. 'Then let us delay no further.'

Edward led her back into the stuffy, overcrowded hospital, unsure how to react to the excitement that surged through him. His life had been lonely, and he had never had any attention from women, his shame at what happened to him as a child and the resulting lack of confidence making even talking to the opposite sex incredibly difficult to the point of crippling. This situation felt different, however. It was a strange feeling for someone to speak to him without prejudice or insulting his appearance. Edward wondered if this was how happiness felt, and if so could see why so many strived to achieve it.

CHAPTER SEVEN

Miller paused, his lower lip trembling as he stared into the fire.

Hapgood set down his pen and stretched. 'You were in love?'

'Very much so, or at least it was the first such experience in my young life at the time. Understand, Mr Hapgood that I had, to that point, lived a life of solitude and hatred, shame and misery. Even George was too busy with his work at the hospital to spend time on our friendship. He was deep into his surgical training funded by the wealth his mother had fallen into and had little time to spend with me. In hindsight, I wonder if he was embarrassed at having a friend mired in the lower classes. It was true that his social class and those he deemed his friends had changed. Gone was the boy who was my childhood ally replaced by a man who had started to wear expensive suits and frequent social gatherings I was neither welcome to and could not afford in any case. Lucy held no such judgement. She and I grew close, first as friends following the demise of her father then as more than that. A bond was growing which neither of us could ignore.'

'What of your… other habits?'

Miller set his empty glass on the table. 'They seemed less important. The urges were still there, yet they were greatly diminished. I killed only two cats and one small dog during that first year of knowing Lucy. I believe if things had continued as they were, you and I would not be conversing here tonight as my life would have taken a different direction. I never imagined my life could recover after the trauma of my childhood and yet Lucy brought out the best in me. Even George commented on one of our rare meetings how the two of us were as one. Always together, our conversations easy and natural. Of course, she could never know my secret. That was for me alone. Even so, nothing good lasts forever and that period of love was to be short lived.'

Hapgood waited for Miller to elaborate, but no more words came. Instead, a deep silence filled the room. 'How about another drink?' Hapgood said, already on his feet and making his way to the drinks cabinet.

'No more brandy for me. I wonder if I could trouble you for some tea?' Miller said, keeping his gaze directed at the fire to hide the tears which ran down his face.

'Of course. Please excuse me for a moment.' Hapgood replied, giving Miller a little privacy to compose himself. He stood in the hall, mind still reeling from the information. It occurred to him he could if he wished, escape. The front door was closer than the kitchen. He could make it to the street and fetch help, tell someone what had happened, but he knew no good would come of it. He would return to find an empty house, and perhaps himself be admonished for wasting the time of the police. Then sometime later, when he was least expecting it, Miller would return and take vengeance for Hapgood's betrayal on both him and his family, and their safety was key in his decision not to flee. More than that, he was now intrigued and invested in the story. There was no evidence of a lie in the things he was being told. His impression was that Miller was who he said he was. The truth of that matter was that he didn't *want* to run. He wanted to hear the rest of the story and know just what had broken the man sitting by his fire and transformed him into the monster he would become. Taking a final look at the door and escape, Hapgood went to the kitchen and began to prepare the tea. He half suspected there was no reason to believe he was in any danger. Whatever Miller once claimed to be, he was now a spent force. A broken shell of what once was. Hapgood decided that he would remain civil and courteous and write Miller's story, true or false he would scribe every last word, and later craft a tremendous book.

'You seem lost in thought, Mr Hapgood.' came the voice from behind him, causing him to spin towards the kitchen door. Miller was watching Hapgood prepare the tea.

'My apologies. I'm sure you can understand this evening has been unusual, to say the least. I am simply processing the information'

'Make no apology Mr Hapgood, it would seem that my trust in you was well served.' He walked into the kitchen and sat at the table. 'You could have escaped if that were your intention, and yet you did not. I wonder why that would be?' Miller was toying with the large bread knife on the table. Hapgood was unable to take his eyes from the blade as it danced and shimmered in the lamplight. Miller saw him watching and laughed. 'This is larger and longer than the one I used,' he said, twisting the knife around and over the back of his hand. 'Too cumbersome for my work.'

Hapgood saw it then. A flash of Hapgood in his prime buried somewhere under the tired and broken thing he was now. The sharpness of the eyes, the wicked half smile as he soaked in his host's fear.

'Have no fear. I mean you no harm. Your discomfort amuses me.' Miller said before plunging the knife into the half loaf of bread and pinning it to the table.

'I would, however, like to know why did you not try to escape? Most would have taken the opportunity to flee.'

Hapgood tried to formulate an excuse, a reasonable lie but could find none. His eyes drifted from the blade to Miller and decided to be truthful. 'Your story is fascinating. I cannot claim to have experienced such horrors as the ones you have confided in me Mr Miller, and although I know that it is wrong to entertain you here in my home if you are who you claim to be. It is true that every fibre in my body tells me to stop…' Hapgood hesitated, looking away from Miller in shame. 'And yet I feel not unsympathetic to your plight, at least so far.' Hapgood finished, before turning back to making the tea.

'There is another reason it is prudent for me to continue. Your notoriety is second to none as you are aware. Telling your story would be good for my future and that of my family. Another opportunity such as this one may never again present itself. I wish to be the one who tells it to the world.'

'And tell it you shall. I also find the evening will be much easier without the fear of escape. It is good that you wish to hear it, Hapgood. Complicity is important.'

Miller picked up the tray containing the tea. 'Shall we return to the study?' Hapgood asked.

Miller shook his head. 'Perhaps we could continue our conversation here for a while?'

Hapgood's eyes went to the knife, still hanging blade from the loaf of bread. Miller followed Hapgood's gaze, the ghost of a smile on his lips.

'Please feel free to put away the knife if it will make you feel more at ease.'

Hapgood flushed and forced himself to look Miller in the eye. 'That won't be necessary,' he said as he set the tea on the table. 'Please help yourself to tea Mr Miller; I will fetch my pen and paper.' When he returned, Miller had poured them both a cup of tea. The bread and knife had been placed by the sink, leaving the kitchen table bare apart from the tea. Hapgood seated himself opposite Miller and prepared his pen and another blank sheet of paper.

'Are you ready to continue?'

Miller sipped his tea and composed his thoughts. 'Yes, I believe I am.' He said as he set his cup on the table. 'So, Lucy and I were together as a couple, our feelings of love confirmed and a beautiful life lay ahead of us. However, I did not account for the trauma of my childhood to have such a profound effect on me. Lucy and I progressed our relationship, and the time came when we were to spend our first night together. Of course, Lucy knew nothing of the terrible deed that I was forced to endure when I was a boy, and so, when the time came, I was unable to consummate our love despite wanting nothing more than to do so. I recall how she said I didn't love her, words born from her lack of understanding of my situation which cut deeper than any wound that my blade could ever inflict. We endeavoured to try of course, and tensions rose further between us with each failure. George and I had almost come to blows after in my frustration the inner rage surfaced and I struck Lucy, an event which even now I regret.' Miller exhaled and placed his palms on the table. 'It's strange Mr Hapgood, despite my awareness of the world around me, I never foresaw what was to come that day in November. Lucy and I had spent another frustrating evening in our bed, trying in vain to consummate our love and move past this barrier which had stifled our relationship.

CHAPTER EIGHT

Tossing back the covers, Lucy climbed out of the bed, crossing to the window unconscious of her naked body.

Edward let his head fall back in frustration, then propped himself up on his elbows.

'I'm sorry.'

'What's wrong with you Edward? Is this not good enough for you?' she said, gesturing to her body. 'Or do you prefer the boys, is that it?' she sneered, as she began to cry.

'Of course not. Please let me try again...'

'Try again?' she screamed at him. 'We have been trying for weeks now Edward and that thing of yours just sits there, slack as you like.' she sat on the bed and refused to look at him. Edward sat up and put a hand on her shoulder, which she shrugged off.

'Don't touch me.' she sobbed. 'Do you not find me attractive?'

'Of course, I do.'

She whirled around jabbing a finger at his bare chest. 'Then why don't you try Edward? Try and explain why you can't get it up for me? What's so wrong with me that you can't even do that?'

'Lucy…' he said, then realised there were no words to follow with. He knew to tell her of his childhood horrors would destroy what remained of their fragile relationship. He opened his mouth to speak, but no words came.

'Just leave me alone,' she screamed at him. 'Just get out and leave me alone.'

Embarrassed and angry, he dressed and opened the door to his lodgings.

'I will take a walk and let you be alone for a while.' He muttered, confidence destroyed. She wouldn't even look at him. With no words to say that would make the situation better, he left. He returned an hour later to find his room dark and empty. Lucy had gone but had not taken her things.

He crossed to the window and looked out into the street. Dusk was close, the streets heavy with long, opaque shadows. He didn't like the thought of her being out alone and from his upbringing knew all too well the kind of dangerous people who frequented Whitechapel after dark. Pulling on his coat, he set out to look for her. He searched for an hour, walking the streets, first down Whitechapel Road, and then towards Spitalfields and some of the public houses there. With each passing moment, he grew more frustrated at the situation. He was desperate to speak to her, to perhaps try and offer an explanation for his failings, but could find no trace of her. He made his way back to his lodgings, and after a quick check to see if Lucy had returned, he left his still empty room and decided to visit George, who he hoped might help him find Lucy.

Already the streets were crowded. Amid the squalor young children played in the filth, their life expectancy ridiculously low and hope for any kind of future even less. Doorways were filled with bodies who were asleep or passed out drunk, others huddled in small groups, chattering and keeping a close eye on everyone who passed. The desperate and the violent crawled out of their daytime hiding places and went about their business aided by the shadows. The less fortunate had already begun to tout for business, offering themselves for a few pennies to anyone who might be interested. Seeing them reminded Edward of his mother. He felt a sudden burst of anger towards these women who sold their dignity for a few pennies. He wished they were dead, every last one of them. Edward turned into Walden Street, fire burning in his belly, the combination of fear and anger making a potent mixture. Here the houses were of better quality, the streets better lit. Just a few streets away sat the Royal London Hospital where he worked, and although a middle-class area, even it could not escape the poverty as the wind would often bring the rancid smell of the slaughterhouses in from the poorer areas which were a little distance away.

Edward arrived at George's home, which was a good sized two-floor building specifically for housing medical students. Edward approached the door and pushed it open then made his way to George's room and going inside. 'George?' he called peering into the empty room. It was barren as was the kitchen. Baffled he paused at the foot of the staircase and a sick and twisted thought popped into his mind. One that thinking about made him nauseous.

He always suspected George had an infatuation with Lucy, and Edward took pride in this being the one thing in which he had the upper hand on his friend after their lives had taken on such different directions. His mind formed images, ideas that George and Lucy were taking him for a fool as George did the things she needed that physically he could not do. His stomach somersaulted as he ascended the steps towards his friend's bedroom.

He knew.

He knew Lucy had fled here, to George. And if she were to whisper in his ear, if she were to tell him about Edward's inability to perform, would George have the will or desire to halt her advances?

As the scenario played out in his mind he could imagine them, writhing and thrashing on the bed, her unleashing her weeks of frustration and him a willing recipient. A sudden and powerful fury overcame him, his cheeks burning hot, his pulse pounding thick in his neck. He walked down the upstairs hallway, bursting into George's room. George lay on the bed, shirtless and reading one of his medical textbooks. 'Edward?'

'Has she been here with you?' Edward screeched, taking a step towards his friend.

George leapt to his feet 'Edward calm down ...'

Edward shoved him aside and looked under the bed.

'I know she has been here George, tell me where she is!' Edward bellowed.

'This is complete madness. I have no idea what you are talking about I...'

Edward spun around and struck his friend hard in the face, sending him stumbling back and onto the bed.

'You tell me where she is, or God help me I'll cut

your fucking throat!' Edward screamed, swiping the stack of books from George's end table, and sending them crashing to the floor.

'You've gone mad!' yelled George, as he touched his bloody lip.

Edward was upon him in an instant, closing his hands around George's throat and pushing him back onto the bed. He squeezed as George clawed at his friend's hands. Edward leaned close, his eyes bulging. 'I see the way you look at her George. I see the way you want her because I have her.'

Edward continued to squeeze, as George flailed and clawed at his friend.

'You think I don't know that every day you think about fucking her?' he screamed; now just inches from his friends face. 'You won't have her. She is mine or she belongs to no-one!' he whispered, as he watched the life begin to fade from his former friend's eyes.

'Edward stop it. Stop it now.' Lucy screamed from behind him. Hearing her voice was akin to someone switching on the lights and allowing him to see what he was doing. He released his grip, stepping back and looking at his own hands, then to George who lay gasping great gulps of air.

She stood in the doorway, her face one of fear and disgust. Edward turned to her, tears streaking his own cheeks.

'Lucy,' he said, holding out his trembling hands to her, dismayed as she took a compensatory step away.

'You animal.' She said, her bottom lip trembling as she walked past him to the bed to comfort George as he struggled to regain his breath.

'You should have been there when I got back. You were gone.' Edward said, backing away towards the door. 'I just wanted you to love me, Lucy.' He added, searching her eyes for any feelings for him which may remain.

'I did love you, Edward, more than anything. But you couldn't love me back. All you had were excuses. I have my needs. You couldn't fulfil them.' She spat at him, her eyes holding now only hatred. He said nothing, trying to keep his thoughts in some kind of rational order.

'George and I have been seeing each other since summer,' she screamed at him, her eyes red and puffy from crying. 'And let me tell you, Edward, he's not like you are downstairs. He's as solid as a rock. At least he's a man. You're just… an animal.' She screamed. Edwards's eyes drifted from his friend to Lucy As he looked at them a cold numbness crept through his body.

'First my mother. Now you,' he mumbled, looking to the floor, and the mess of books.

'You whore,' he said as he looked her in the eye. 'You fucking whore.' he screamed at her, so loudly that she shrank against George who himself winced away from his former friend. Edward felt a heat build within him, a fury unlike any he had ever experienced before. He slammed his fist into the door, splintering the wood panel and leaving a great bloody gash on his forearm. He glared at them now, his eyes filled with a hatred so intense that neither one of them could look him in the eye. Without uttering another word, he turned and left the house.

CHAPTER NINE

Miller stood and walked to the kitchen window, looking out at the shadow filled yard beyond. The snow which had threatened had regressed back to rain which left streaks on the window where it landed. Hapgood had seen the pain in Miller's eyes and knew speaking about it had taken a tremendous toll on him.

'The following weeks were somewhat of a daze, Hapgood, and unfortunately, I cannot recall specific details of that dark time to relay back to you as part of this story. I know my frustration and sorrow were quelled somewhat by my kills which escalated to proportions never before indulged. I knew even then that rats and dogs would not long satisfy my growing desires. My hatred for whores was cemented on that day. They are filthy creatures, Hapgood. Women, I mean. Carriers of disease and illness who use sex to manipulate a man. I was still a young man and yet stood alone in a world which had shunned me and left me confused and broken. A man without direction. Is it any surprise knowing what you do now that my journey took the course it did?'

Hapgood looked up from his writing. 'Despite my sympathy to your ordeal, I cannot condone or justify your later actions.'

Miller turned to face his host, a curious smile on his lips. 'How so Mr Miller? All women had ever brought to me was misery. The world would be a better place without them. You cannot possibly understand Mr Hapgood, not in the fullest sense anyway. The words as I tell them have a certain impact, but even that pales in comparison to actually having to live through those experiences. Yes, life has indeed been cruel to me. First my mother then Lucy and later, as you will learn, there were other situations which did all they could to push me towards the path I was desperate to resist. Of course, will can only help for a certain length of time and I made a decision. The world had decided to show me how cruel it could be and so, in return, I responded with cruelty to it and took my vengeance on those who had wronged me.'

'Are you saying you hold no regret for the slaughter of those women even now after the passage of so many years?' Hapgood asked.

'What is to regret? Instead of being hounded and called a monster I should have been commended. By ridding the streets of those filthy disgusting creatures I was acting with the best of intentions. A great work indeed for the good of everyone.'

'That is a fiendish justification. One I cannot agree with.'

'You have no right to judge me. You are here only to record the facts. To be impartial in the telling. My judgement will come soon enough from God, and I will stand before him without shame nor fear if I am to be held accountable for my great work.' Miller sneered.

'I fear that you will stand not before God but the devil himself, and perhaps even he will deem you too evil for hell and return you to earth.'

Miller smiled. 'Perhaps… and yet here you are Hapgood, drinking tea with the man you deem too evil for the devil himself. I wonder, does that make you as bad, if not worse a monster than I?'

Miller returned to his seat and folded his hands in front of him. He focused his stare on Hapgood, enjoying watching the writer squirm under his gaze.

'George and Lucy would go on to marry, and the last I heard of them, they moved to Yorkshire and have two children. Neither of them spoke to me again of course, and as far as I know, George made no complaint of my assault of him. I started to receive money from them, however. Regular amounts which were generous, certainly far more than I could earn through my lowly position at the hospital. I suspect guilt drove them to it, perhaps by way of apology for their betrayal. Nonetheless, I took the money if only because I could not bear to make contact with them again to inquire as to its purpose. The thought of seeing either of them again filled me with an all consuming dread like no other.

And so we separated. George and Lucy to their new life together, myself mired in the desperation of Whitechapel. For a time, I was a ship without anchor lost in a sea of darkness. I began to have dreams, Hapgood, twisted dark visions of flesh flayed from bone, of skinless women, lined single file as far as the eye could see waiting to enter the slaughterhouse. Dreams of blood running the cobbled streets of London. These would occur later in my life as we will cover in due course. However back then those visions terrified me as I did not understand their meaning. I would wake in the dark of my lodgings biting my fist to avoid screaming into the night. It was one of these nights, restless and unable to find sleep that the next stage of my journey found me. Unwilling to endure any more of my dreams, I dressed and set out onto the heart of Whitechapel. I liked to walk back then, Hapgood. Unfortunately, I have since developed problems with my knees which mean that I am not quite as mobile as I once was. Back then, however, I would walk everywhere, taking in the sights, and the sounds, even the smells of the filthy streets around me, feeling at home with the wretches and the scum, the poor and the destitute. The hopeless. I was, after all, one of them. Unlike George, I had never escaped it. Take up your pen, Mr Hapgood. There is much more of this story yet to tell.

CHAPTER TEN

Even at such a late hour, Whitechapel teemed with life. The church clock signalled three in the morning yet still children scurried and played, as their mothers drunk and tottered, leaning on their equally drunk friends as they bellowed at passers-by or tried to solicit themselves for a few pennies. Edward walked the streets, head down, hands thrust in pockets. He ignored the jeers, the jibes, and the incessant chatter. Ahead of him, a brawl broke out in a doorway between two men which spilled into the street followed by a few interested spectators. Edward walked on paying no mind. His mood had turned dark, darker even than the deepest recesses of the dimly lit passages and streets which surrounded him and a long forgotten voice was beginning to whisper to him from within. His eyes flitted to the whores. He watched as they indulged in whispered conversation with their customers, before retreating to a dark and unseen place to complete the transaction. Anger filled him, an all-consuming hatred which was becoming familiar.

'You want the business?' came a slurred voice from behind him.

Edward looked the woman up and down as she peered from the archway, his expression not betraying the burning rage that she had dared address him. She was overweight, her filthy brown hair pulled back in a scraggly clump on her head. Her small features were drawn and under her left eye was the yellowish remains of a recent bruise. Her skin looked strange to Edward, pale and lifeless. Her flabby hands went to her hips as she tried to strike a seductive pose. Edward almost laughed at the idiocy but was somehow able to retain his demeanour.

'You look lost, love. I can maybe help you find something for just three pennies.'

Edward said nothing, doing all he could to quell

his disgust.

'As it happens I have a few pennies to spend.' Edward heard himself saying, feeling as if he were some kind of a passenger in his own body. The prostitute grinned, revealing what remained her decayed teeth.

'Come on then love, this way,' she said before shrinking back into the blackness of the archway. Edward looked around the busy streets, yet nobody paid any attention. He noted that he was no different to the scores of other people here, and his actions were of no interest to them. He walked into the archway, the smell of filth and desperation causing him to wrinkle his nose. There was no light, Edward taking a moment to allow his eyes to adjust to the darkness. The archway extended for another ten feet beyond her, then turned to the right. The passageway was otherwise unoccupied.

'This way love,' came her voice from the dark as Edward began to walk towards her. He could see her now, a vague shape in the darkness for which Edward was grateful.

'Gimmie a second just to hitch up my skirts love,' she said as he approached, her rancid breath even fouler smelling than the alleyway. His heart raced, yet it was not with sexual excitement, it was the thought of what he could do to this woman, the control he had over her. He wondered what her innards would look like, and imagined his hands dripping with blood. The vision was so clear, so sharp that it thrilled him.

'Come on then love, lets ave ya,' she said, turning her back and exposing her filthy lower body to him. He approached, breath coming in great gasps as he tried to control himself.

'You sound ready for this love. Go on then, put it in.'

He put his hands on the wall either side of her head and stood close, his chest almost touching her back. He was looking at her neck, imagining how it would feel when he wrapped his hands around it. Just as he was about to commit, another couple stumbled into the alleyway. Edward recoiled, glaring at the couple as they stumbled towards them

'Sorry,' said the drunk man as he stumbled past followed by another prostitute, this one waif thin and filthy. Edward backed away, pressing his back against the opposite wall.

'You ok love?' Said the prostitute as she walked past Edward, looking him up and down.

Edward looked her in the eye, then his gaze drifted to the corner where the woman he had almost killed was frowning.

'Don't worry about those two, come on. Let's finish up,' she said, again flashing her horrible grin. Edward looked at his hands, thinking about what he had almost done.

Without a word, he walked away, heading out of the alleyway. At some point he started to run, making his way through the side streets and back home. He wept until the sun rose, then dried his face and stood at the door of his lodgings, looking up and down the street which was still silent apart from those heading to work, the hazy blue pink hue of the rising sun filtering through the smog giving a beautiful quality to the morning, and with it clarity of thought for the first time since Lucy had betrayed him. He knew at that instant what he must do to bring peace to his mind. Closing the door, he moved to the desk in his room, and opened the drawer, taking out the package which lay inside. He turned the parcel over in his hands. It was a gift for George which he and Lucy had bought for when he graduated from the medical university and became a fully-fledged doctor. Edward tore open the package. Inside was a smaller, box, black with a brass latch.

The knife which lay inside was quite beautiful. The blade was solid steel and around six inches long. The handle black and offering good grip. Edward lifted the blade, enjoying the weight in his hand. He looked at the steel, the way it reflected his face, warping his features into a close approximation of how he felt inside. He had hoped that holding the blade might deter him from the idea that was forming in his mind, yet the effect was the opposite. It felt good as he wielded it, it felt right. Unlike the women who had destroyed his life, it would never betray or fail him. It would be strong for him as long as he was strong enough to use it. He touched the blade edge, slicing his finger with barely a touch. He would not allow his life to be destroyed by any more filthy whores, both his mother and Lucy would be responsible for what was about to occur. He would strike without mercy and the streets would run red with the blood of all whores. For the first time, he felt a sense of purpose, a direction, and a confidence that he would be able to achieve the thing which he desired most. Revenge would be his and be paid in blood. He lay on his bed and closed his eyes, seeing in his mind the carnage, the fear he would generate. He would give himself a name. Something they would never forget and which would soon be on the lips of all whores and he would do it with the knife bought for the friend who had betrayed him. The tool of a man who would save lives would be his instrument to take them.

For the first time in weeks, he slept soundly.

CHAPTER ELEVEN

Hapgood hesitated, knowing they had reached the part of the story he was least looking forward to documenting. 'It was here it began, then?'

'Yes, although not in the sense that you know it.'

'How so?'

'I was young and full of ideas but knew little of how I might go about such deeds even though I knew my work must begin. I had continued to frequent the places where the filthy whores would be found, cavorting and squealing. With each passing day, my rage grew until one day that which I had known to be coming for so long, finally happened.'

Hapgood referred to his notes 'This would be the Nichols woman, on the thirty-first of August.' Hapgood said.

'Actually, no, Mr Hapgood.'

'I don't understand.'

'The general thoughts within the press and from the police were that my work began on that day late in August. In actuality, it began earlier that month. I wanted to test my abilities before starting my work proper. My lust for revenge was strong, Hapgood, but I was not yet ready to announce myself to the world. After all, thinking about the work I intended to begin was much different from the physical act. I knew I needed to test myself, to see if I had the will to match the desire. And so, Early in August, I set out into the night to the streets that had become so familiar to me I thought of them as my home.

CHAPTER TWELVE

The Two Brewers public house teemed with life.

Situated on the corner of Brick Lane, it was filled with singing and loud conversation by its patrons, most of which were intoxicated. Edward sat in the corner, watching the mass of humanity and feeling disgust and disassociation at how vile they were. As he observed, his eyes drifted to the two women at the bar who were indulged in raucous conversation with two soldiers. They looked out of place here, their red uniforms too bright, too vibrant compared to the rest of the clientele. They had no doubt come into port on one of the many vessels which docked in London, taking shore leave to drink and womanise before boarding the ship again and going on their way. Edward watched as the two women flaunted themselves at the soldiers, exposing their flesh to them, whispering in their ears and bellowing in drunken laughter. Edward sipped his beer, watching the disgusting and vulgar display in front of him. They reminded him of his mother, another whore who had ruined his life. A group of men at the table beside him had begun to argue, their words slurred by too much alcohol. Edward was barely able to concentrate and was developing a headache. Finishing his drink, he stood and pushed his way through the crowd, passing within just a few feet of the two women who looked at him as he passed.

'Ere Martha,' said the scrawnier of the two 'That one there was lookin' at you.'

The larger woman, overweight, and eyes glazed with drink cackled and slurred back

'He can wait his turn, Polly love. The officer ere' is more my type anyway.'

Edward ignored them pushed his way through the door and outside, immediately grateful for both the quiet and the cool air in comparison to the sticky heat of the pub. He walked across the road then taking a position where he could observe the doors stood in the shadows and waited. People bustled and scurried, some were already passed out in doorways or leaning against walls. Even from his position across the street, he could still hear the chatter and noise. His headache had grown into a thunderous throbbing migraine and those inner voices were shouting to make themselves heard. He could stand it no longer and was about to leave when he saw the women and the soldiers stumble out of the pub. They stood outside for a few moments, the women hopelessly drunk, the soldiers not quite so. They began to walk down the street, their drunken chatter coming to Edward in snatches.

He followed them, keeping to the shadows. It was sometime later when the quartet staggered out of the White Swan pub, now all so drunk they could barely walk. Edward watched as they prepared to go their separate ways, enjoying the hunt and the thrill of the chase.

'Martha, this gentleman has lost something that perhaps I can help him to find.' the thinner woman said, with a drunken grin.

'I'll see you later Polly,' replied her equally drunken friend. 'This handsome chap is also looking for a warm place aren't you love?' she said, nudging the soldier and trying her best to look seductive.

Polly took her soldier by the arm. 'I might see

you back in the Bells later then,' she said, leading her man away.

'That you might' replied Martha, heading in the opposite direction. Edward followed them, still at a distance as the pair made their way through the warren-like streets of Whitechapel. They were approaching Wentworth Street, an area that Edward knew well from his nights walking and lost in thought. The pair stopped outside the entrance to George's Yard buildings. Edward smiled at the irony. The yard which shared the name of his former friend who took Lucy from him. It would be a perfect place to begin his campaign. Approaching the archway which turned off from Whitechapel road, he continued to watch. The pair had a short conversation before Martha led the soldier into the archway. Edward followed, peering around the corner, the shadows so black he was completely out of sight. He could see them on the first-floor landing. Her skirts were hitched up high, as the soldier, his trousers down around his feet furiously thrust away at her.

Edward thought back to his mother, then to Lucy. His hand went to his pocket and the knife wrapped in linen which lay within. He waited patiently as the soldier grunted his way to climax.

'How was that for ya love?' Martha said as she readjusted her skirts.

'Just what I needed at the end of a pleasant night.' Replied the soldier, handing over a shilling to Martha.

'Thank you kindly, sir,' she said, but he was already leaving, the transaction complete. Edward pushed himself into the darkness, and the soldier walked past him without pausing, nor noticing his presence. He waited for a moment, then came out of the shadows, walking up the few steps towards her. She glanced at him, flashing a drunken smile.

'Ello darlin. You like what you see?' she asked, exposing a flabby, pendulous breast. He said nothing.

'I saw you in the Bells earlier didn't I love? Watchin' me you were.' She tried to look seductive, but Edward saw the desperation in her which further increased his anger and roused the voice that lived deep within his mind.

Bitch whore.

He nodded then spoke. 'Are we safe here?' he asked, looking around the deserted hallway.

'Oh don't you worry love, nobody will disturb us. Come on, get it out and let's get on.' She said as she leant forwards to hitch up her filthy skirt. He couldn't believe how easy she had made it for him. He reached into his jacket and pulled out the knife, quickly unwrapping it. He took a step toward her and thrust the knife at her, the blade slipping through her chest with less resistance than he anticipated. She tried to scream but could let out only a dry gasp as she staggered back to the wall, and fell to the ground on her side. Looking around to ensure he was alone, Edward rolled her onto her back, and gazed into her eyes, watching the life dim, and then fade. In that moment, she was his mother. She was Lucy. Fury overcame him and he began to drive the knife into her, over and over again, the consumption by the rage total. He lost count of how many times he stabbed her, only stopping when his arm became too tired to continue. He slid away from her, panting with exertion. There was less blood than he anticipated. He knew many whores were without permanent lodgings and wore everything they had as they walked the streets, near homeless. Those layers had done a fine job of soaking up much of the blood. Even so, there was still some evidence of his work. His hands shook and he felt an overwhelming sense of power at his deed. He looked at her now, her body twisted and mangled and he realised that he felt nothing. No remorse, no sadness. Just a euphoria and satisfaction.

He cleaned his blade on an unstained section of her green skirt then rewrapped it and placed it back in his jacket. Standing, he made to leave and then paused.

He knew the soldier had just paid this woman for sex, and that he had been seen with her for most of the night. With a smile, he returned to the body, arching her legs and pushing them aside, as if intercourse had taken place on the ground. He stepped back, admiring his work, and then, hearing voices approaching, he hid around the corner of the following ascending stairway, holding his breath as he waited. The voices grew louder, then passed the entrance and receded into the distance. He looked at his hands, which were smeared with blood, as was the front of his shirt. He exited the building and began to make his way deeper into Whitechapel. He felt elated, a great weight removed from his shoulders. He had anticipated that it would be difficult, but the whores were too willing, and he was all too eager. They knew the places to go where there would be no disturbance. Upon returning home without incident he looked at himself in the mirror. His face was mostly clean apart from a few spots of blood. Not bothering to clean it off, he pleasured himself, able for the first time to feel arousal at the sight of himself drenched in blood. When he was finished he drew a hot bath, and as he soaked he replayed the events in his head. How bold could he be? How big a risk could he take to ensure maximum fear? Could he do it in crowded places where the bodies were likely to be found quickly and still warm? If so could he escape without detection?

Yes.

Many questions indeed that required answers. But not tonight. Tonight he had worked enough. He yawned, the warm water bringing with it a fatigue. His shoulder burned with the fury of his work, yet it was a good pain. He likened it to the satisfied ache of a man who had done an honest day's work and decided that next time, he would see the insides. He would open them up and spill them on the streets for all to see. He yawned, and climbed out of his bath, checking his watch. It was almost six in the morning. Making his way into the bedroom, he dried and then lay down, closing his eyes. He wondered if they had found the body yet and if so what they would think of his handiwork. He let his thoughts drift, as he lapsed into a dreamless sleep. For the next few days, he scanned the newspapers for word on his work but was underwhelmed by its lack of coverage. The realisation came to him that if he were to really strike fear into the people then he would have to do more. Whores were routinely found dead. It was a danger of their work. For him to stand out he would have to do more. He would need to make sure he was remembered.

His mood was cheerful as he made his way to work, the night air crisp and fresh. Although not his usual route, he went out of his way to pass the archway leading to George's yard. As he passed he looked down the narrow passage but saw nothing out of the ordinary. He had hoped to see crowds of onlookers pointing and whispering, yet aside from a stray dog sniffing about the waste piled against the wall, there was no activity. Frustrated and angry, he made his way over Whitechapel road through a narrow passageway and towards the Hospital. His anger although satisfied for the time being still lingered within him. He marvelled at how easy it had been. Whitechapel was the perfect environment to complete his work, and so he would do another, and another. He missed Lucy terribly, yet the thought of her betrayal renewed his lust for revenge. He arrived at the hospital early for his shift, and so he skirted around the building, heading for the quiet of the enclosed garden area. He had developed another headache and here was the place he would often come to find solace. When he arrived he found that he was not alone. He drew breath as he looked upon the horrifically disfigured individual who stood before him. His face was covered with bony nodules, his body twisted leaving the man unable to walk upright. Edward had heard of this man, a resident of the hospital named Joseph Merrick, however, this was the first time he himself had set eyes upon the pitiful creature.

'I'm sorry to disturb you,' said Edward, lowering his gaze.

'Please, do not leave on my account, I rarely have company.' replied Merrick.

Edward found it hard to understand the words,

Merrick's jaw and mouth and resulting disfigurement making it difficult for him to speak. The poor wretch had been given the awful title of the Elephant Man and was used as a circus sideshow freak for those willing to pay to see him. In actuality, Joseph was incredibly warm and intelligent and compassionate even to those who exploited him since birth. Edward looked upon this man and realised that he was on the outside how Edward felt within, twisted and disfigured. He noted with interest that they were opposites.

'Mr Merrick I believe?' Edward said, holding out his hand. Merrick looked back in wonder and shook it.

'You are not repulsed by me?' Merrick asked.

'Not at all, Sir. My repulsion is reserved for those who treat you with such disrespect.'

'Are you a visitor here at the hospital?'

'No, sir. I work here.'

Merrick nodded, as he and Edward began to walk the gardens.

'I do not blame them for how they treat me. It is

human nature to be afraid of that which they do not understand,' Merrick said. Edward could hear his breath, coming in great wet rasps.

'I too walk alone, Mr Merrick. And yet now I fear a path is laid before me from which I cannot turn back.'

'Our fate is inevitable.' Said Merrick. 'Each of us must go on the journey set out for us by God.'
'I'm afraid I lost my faith in God some time ago, Mr Merrick.'

Merrick stopped, and turned to Edward, peering at him with his one visible eye

'You should retain your faith. We are defined by the things that we do. Our time here is short, and soon we will be forgotten unless we make ourselves remembered.'

'I tried to make myself noticed in the world, Mr Merrick, and yet still my work was ignored,' Edward replied as the pair began to walk again. For a time, there was silence between them

'As you can see by my appearance, I can only step outside my room after dark for fear of frightening the public. Because of this, my days are long, and without something to fill them I fear I would go quite mad. A mind without focus can be dangerous,' said Merrick, astounding Edward with his articulation and intelligence. 'If you feel passion for the work you do, then do not let one setback stop you. Do not wait until it is too late, or you will regret the time wasted.'

Edward nodded. 'Thank you, Joseph,' he said gratefully. 'I know now what I must do.'

'I have enjoyed our conversation, it is rare that I converse with anyone but Mr Treves, and he only visits on a Sunday,' said Merrick.

'I would like to visit you again if you would be willing to see me of course.'

'I would very much like that.' Said Merrick.

'As would I, Sir. You have renewed my faith in my ability.' Edward said shaking hands with Merrick, making sure he held out his left hand in order to receive Merrick's right, which was without deformity. 'I wish I could stay and speak with you longer but I must go to work.'

'I shall be here when you wish to speak again. I hope you find renewed faith in your work. If it is something you are passionate for then you should ensure nothing stops you from achieving it.'

'May I ask what is it you desire, Mr Merrick? From life I mean?'

Merrick considered the question. 'Fate has given me this deformity and so every day is a gift to me. I know my face makes people afraid and it saddens me. I do understand it, however. Fear breeds. It passes from person to person like a plague. My fear and my passion are one and the same. Because of my face and the weight of my bone deformity, I sleep propped upright in the corner of my bed. My wish is something which to you seems quite ordinary. I long to lie down and sleep like a normal person with my head on a pillow even though I know I can never do this as to do so would bring death. One day, when I deem I have seen enough of this world I will do just that. I will sleep like a regular person and let death take me. Do not give up on your dreams, Mr Miller. Follow them and live without regret.'

'I will. Thank you again, Joseph. It was an honour to make your acquaintance.' Edward turned and left, heading inside the hospital to begin his shift.

CHAPTER THIRTEEN

Miller paused, lost in contemplation. Hapgood wrote on, ignoring the screaming in his wrist and the numb feeling in his fingers. He was breathless, and at first didn't realise that Miller had stopped speaking. He finished writing, and then looked at Miller.

'This is incredible, who would think that the elephant man would...'

'Joseph,' Miller interrupted. 'His name was Joseph and he was a wonderful man.'

Hapgood lowered his gaze, realising how cold it was in the room.

'I apologise. It was him then, Mr Merrick who spurred you on to continue?'

'Not knowingly. His advice was with the best of intentions I'm sure.'

'Indeed. And you took to visiting him regularly I presume?' he added.

Miller shook his head.

'Sadly not. If I have one regret then this is it. I intended to, of course, however as the next months progressed, I'm sorry to say poor Joseph slipped my mind as thoughts of my work consumed me.'

Hapgood said nothing, feeling that silence was the best response.

'I do miss him, Mr Hapgood. When news of his passing reached me, I felt genuine sadness. I wish I had visited him once more. I understand he did as he told me that evening in the gardens. When he was ready he lay down and embraced death as it came.'

There was a lengthy silence, and then Hapgood

stood and stretched.

'Perhaps now would be a good time to take a short break.'

'I fear that if I stop now then I will not be able to continue. I...'

He began to cough, producing a white handkerchief from his pocket and holding it over his mouth and nose. Eventually, it subsided, and Miller wiped his lips. The handkerchief was stained with blood.

'Do not be alarmed,' Miller said folding the handkerchief back into his pocket.

'My death is approaching and unavoidable. Perhaps now you now understand the urgency of my meeting with you?'

It was as if seeing this man coughing up blood in his kitchen shattered the myth that Hapgood had built. He was just a man, one who suddenly looked very old and frail. Hapgood was sure he could stand and walk away, and Miller would not try to stop him. Yet as much as he hated himself for it, he wanted to hear the rest, even though he knew something of the brutality to come.

'You see me differently. The monster's death draws close and his aura dies with him.'

Hapgood looked at the table, unsure what to say.

'I understand. To this world, I am a beast. A vile thing that any man would say deserves his death. Yet you still want to hear my story. What came next. What came after that which you know.'

'I know how this story ends. You forget I was working on my book before you came to my door this evening.'

'The Kelly woman? You believe that to be the end? That was just a chapter, a stop on a road which will yet grow more twisted before my story is finished. As I said when I arrived, Hapgood. Forget all you think you know. You have heard only a small segment of this particular story.'

A silence, heavy and oppressive fell over the kitchen. The rain continued it's incessant tapping on the kitchen window trying to get in.

'Perhaps we should move back into the study?' Hapgood suggested.

'Yes, it grows cold this night Hapgood. And the tale will grow colder yet.'

Hapgood nodded and scooped up the stack of paper he had written on, and carried them to the study. Miller followed, veering towards the window which looked out onto the slushy streets. Hapgood sat at his desk, refilling the inkwell, which had almost run dry.

'Tis a cold winter is it not Mr Hapgood?'

'Indeed, it is.'

Miller returned to his seat, and Hapgood waited, pushing thoughts of the moralistic rights or wrongs of what he was doing to one side.

Without warning, Miller continued his tale. 'It was August, eighteen eighty-eight. It had been a little over two weeks since my discussion with Joseph and with my renewed determination only increased by the filthy whores selling their rancid flesh on the streets I was ready to strike again. I had chosen the twenty-ninth, the anniversary of the day I found out the truth about my whore of a mother. A fitting day indeed. History states I had actively selected the next whore as my first; however, her fate was decided by the filthy stinking bitch herself and I only happened upon her by chance after an earlier failed attempt. As with the first, I was watching from the corner of the Ten Bells which at that time was a veritable nest of those vile and filthy women.

CHAPTER FOURTEEN

Set at the corner of Commercial Street and Fournier Street, The Ten Bells was a popular location for the lower classes of Whitechapel. The small building was full and on most nights its patrons would linger in the doorways or lean on the walls outside as they drank and smoked. Edward sat inside, his table offering him a good view of the door and the bar. It was loud and hot, the air stinking of humanity and alcohol. He finished his fourth drink of the evening and was beginning to feel a little the worse for it as he watched the people who stood in groups laughing and talking, their inhibitions diminished by the alcohol they had consumed. He rubbed his temples, trying to block out the symphony of noise which barraged his senses and refocused his attention to the bar and the two women he had been watching since he arrived, his fury growing with each passing moment. Both had been desperate in their attempts to sell themselves to every man who walked through the door. Edward thought the younger of the two was quite attractive for a whore. Her blonde hair fell below the shoulders and she had an almost innocent face which was betrayed by the way she leaned on the bar, one hand on her hip, chest pushed out and offering what she had to anyone who might be interested.

The other woman was much older and appeared hideous next to her companion. She was overweight, her hair pulled back on her skull. When she laughed he saw she was missing most of her front teeth.

Amid the smell of smoke and yeast, he was even more certain it was because of women like this that people like him were condemned to suffer. He could imagine them, spreading their diseased and ravaged bodies to anyone willing to throw a few pennies at them and wondered how many lives they had ruined, how many lives like his had been destroyed by whores who cared nothing for the consequences of their actions.

He would fix it. He would cleanse the city and purge it of its disease. He would strike and strike again until the streets ran red with the blood with no fear of the consequences if he were caught. He knew God was on his side and would see to it that his work was completed. Pushing his simmering rage aside he stood and made his way towards the bar, shoving his way into a gap beside the two women.

'Same again?' asked the barkeeper, a barrel of a man with whiskers and a large overhanging stomach.

Edward nodded as he handed over his empty glass. He glanced at the two women, their respective beauty and ugliness more apparent up close.

He could smell the desperation on them, the disease which ravaged them to the core.

'You ok love?' The older of the two had asked, flashing her toothless grin at him.

Resisting the urge to tear out her eyes he nodded and smiled knowing the game had begun.

'I am, thank you. Would you two ladies like a drink?'

'Thank you, that is most kind of you.' The younger of the two said. Edward thought she looked a lot like Lucy. They shared similar features. He turned back to the bar, motioning to the barkeep to pour two more pints of ale.

'Two beautiful ladies such as yourselves should not be drinking alone in a place like this. My name is Edward Miller. And you are?'

The younger of the two women took his hand and shook it. 'My name is Mary, and this is my friend Polly.'

Edward nodded to Polly, staring at the plump rolls of flesh on her arms and wondering how easy it would rip at the end of his blade.

'Pleasure to meet you both.'

'So old cock, do you come here often? I don't think I've seen you here before.' Polly said. She was slurring her words and struggling to stay on her feet.

'No, I'm new to the area. I'm out to see what Whitechapel has to offer.'

Polly cackled and nudged Mary 'You came to the right place love, lots on offer round 'ere, if you know where to look, ain't' there, Mary love?'

Mary nodded and looked at Edward. 'Aye, always a lot happening here that's for sure.'

Polly leaned close, her breath putrid with booze and decay. 'If you are lookin' for something in particular, perhaps we can help you find it for a penny or two.'

Edward was about to respond when she lost her footing and tumbled into a table, tipping it over and falling to the ground in a symphony of broken glass. A cheer erupted from the rowdy crowd as Polly struggled to get back to her feet.

The barkeeper pointed at Polly who was sitting on the floor and laughing to herself.

'Polly Nichols, get yourself up and out of here. I'm not avin' you staggering about drunk and smashing the place up.'

'Fuck off John, I lost my footing that's all, 'she screeched as she stood, still tottering. She propped herself on the bar, using it to stop herself from taking another tumble.

'I don't care, come on, Out.'

'John Waldron, I shall take my business elsewhere,' she slurred as she staggered to the door.

Waldren shook his head and returned to his customers leaving Kelly and Edward alone.

'Your friend seems a little worse for the drink,' Edward said.

'She likes a drink, that's for sure.'

'Your accent... Scottish?' he asked.

'Irish. I was born there and moved over to England when I was just a girl. Things didn't work out quite as I expected. I didn't think the accent was still there.' She said, lowering her gaze and taking a sip of her drink. She looked up to find Edward staring at her.

'What is it?' she asked.

'You remind me of someone I once knew.'

'Perhaps after this drink, you and I can go

somewhere and speak in private?'

He sipped his drink, trying to appear casual as he gripped his glass tight enough to turn his knuckles white. 'I'm afraid I must decline your offer. I would, however, like you to stay and drink with me.'

He wasn't sure why he said it. He would be unable to complete his work until he got the whore outside and away from the crowd, and yet her similarity to Lucy was stirring old and long forgotten memories and making him once again question if the path he had chosen was one he was willing and able to complete.

'It's unusual for a gentleman to ask simply for conversation,' Mary said as she took another sip of her drink.

'As I said already, Miss, I wish to find out more of the area in which I am to work.'

'Well, to tell the truth, what you see is what you get. People here are mostly poor. Take me for example, I'm a good person, truly I am. I'm just down on my luck.'

'You are ...'

Stinking filthy whore.

'... An unfortunate aren't you Miss Kelly?'

Embarrassed, she lowered her gaze.

'At least call it what it is. I'm a whore. I do what I have to so I can get by. It doesn't mean I like it.

Edward's inward battle between guilt and fury raged on. 'I apologise if I offended you.'

'Times are difficult. I don't like the things I have to do in order to survive any more than you do by the expression on your face.'

'I understand. All of us do what we must in this world. Perhaps one day your fortunes will change.'

'I would like to think so, however, I do not yet see an end to my situation. I've been here for three years now, in Whitechapel I mean. Of course, I do better than some, Poly is always worse for drink. I fear I'll become like her.'

He wanted to tell her not to worry, that it was the fate of all women to offer their stinking, festering fuck holes to any man willing to pay, and that she, like them, would be better off dead. The moralistic and guilt-ridden side of him which had fought so valiantly had now retreated, leaving the cold black festering thing in charge once more. He was conscious of the number of people that had seen him here and cursed them. If he were to tear the flesh from this one later that night, it would surely lead back to him and his work would be over before it even began. Instead, he smiled at her. Choosing words he knew comfort her.

'If I may say so miss, I see you as different to most of the other unfortunates of Whitechapel. You are beautiful and well spoken. I'm sure you will one day find that your suffering will be over.'

But not this night little whore. My Lucy will wait to get hers for a while yet.

'I appreciate the kind words Sir and hope you are right. I've had enough of living like this.'

Edward was struggling to focus. His eyes drifted to the apron she was wearing. He imagined it soaked with her blood, how brilliantly bright it would look. He wanted badly to kill her, the desire to tear her flesh was almost too much to bear and knew he must leave lest he do it there and then.

'I'm afraid I must go. The hour grows late.

She nodded, and moved towards him, whispering in his ear. 'Are you certain you need no company tonight Mr Miller?'

He saw in her eyes a feral desire and wondered if she perhaps thought he would take her in and offer her the life which she dreamed of. He did want to take her home, yet couldn't decide if he wanted to kill her or build a rapport, get her away from the wretched stench and squalor and see if she could provide that which Lucy couldn't and stop the path which until earlier that night had seemed like the only option available to him. He was suddenly very aware of the volume of chatter coming from all around as he breathed the smoky, stale air which burned his lungs.

'Again I must decline. I would, however, like to see you again,' he blurted before he could stop himself. The rage in his gut was hot and he felt as if he were going to explode.

'I would like that.' She said but elaborated no

further.

He shook her hand, both repulsed and elated at her touch and made his leave, pushing outside into the night. Rain poured with fury, but he was grateful for the cool air on his skin. His head drummed at the same pace as his heart as the conflict within him poked and prodded at his psyche. He walked past the church at Spitalfields, hoping that air and distance would help him to resolve such an unexpected conflict. Almost every street was filled with people crammed into the narrow warrens like animals. He passed a filthy and decrepit old man who sat on the edge of the road, shaking and muttering to himself oblivious of the rain.

Edwards mind swam with images of blood, and tearing flesh from Mary's body, her face in his mind pulsing and changing, first to Lucy, and then to his mother and back to Mary. He made his way onto old Montague Street. Here, at last, it was quieter, the dense population on the streets thinning considerably. He saw a familiar figure in front of him. It was Mary's friend, Polly. She was staggering towards him, hopelessly drunk yet somehow still upright. She wore a bonnet offering some protection from the rain, which had begun to ease. She walked past him, lost in a drunken stupor.

'Polly,' he said, unsure he was going to speak until the words had come.

She turned around, looking at him with glazed eyes until recognition struck her. 'Ello, love. I didn't expect to see you out here,' she slurred.

'I'm lost, and wondered if you were still willing to help me find what I'm looking for,' he said, the inner rage now in control and driving his actions.

She cackled, tottering on her feet. 'You come with me love. I'll show you where to go,'

She turned and walked on ahead of him, crossing the road at St. Marys Street and continuing down Montague Street. The fury in him was alive, a living entity of its own.

'Is there nowhere quiet we can go?' he asked.

'Don't you worry about that love, I know just the place.' She reached the end of the street and turned right, walking a short while and then turning off onto Durward Street. The street was deserted.

That's it, whore, find us a nice quiet place where we can be alone

'How's this for ya, my love? Always quiet down 'ere. Three times tonight I've had my money for a doss and spent it on drink,' she chuckled as she staggered down the street.

She turned to him, leaning drunk against a wooden fence which led to a stable.

'Come on then love, let's be 'avin' ya.' She said.

There was no thought. No hesitation or panic. He lunged, grasping her plump neck with both hands. She let out a startled gasp as she clawed at his chest. A surge of adrenaline coursed through him as he squeezed tighter. Her eyes were now no longer glazed with drink, but sober and filled with terror. She went limp, her legs buckling from under her as he lowered her down beside the stable door. She was still breathing, a solitary wheeze coming from her throat.

'I hope you can hear me, whore,' he whispered

as he pulled the wrap containing his knife from his pocket.

'You filthy, dirty cunt,' he whispered as he knelt beside her.

He gripped the blade and slashed her throat from the left towards him, a jet of blood squirting from her neck. She gargled, and one leg twitched. He was filled with a burst of energy, as he took the blade to the opposite side of the neck, and pulled it across with all the force he could muster, the blade cutting through the flesh and muscles with ease. He felt the blade catch on the bones of the neck even as a great gout of blood bubbled upwards and spilt over onto the pavement.

'And now, whore, a fitting end to your filthy life,' he whispered as he pulled up her skirts, exposing her fatty stomach. He made three downward slashes, watching as the skin separated. With images of his mother in his mind, he plunged the knife in below her ribs and pulled the blade towards him opening a deep incision which began to seep blood from the fatty, yellow inner skin.

'A little surprise for those that find you, whore,' he whispered as he made a few further slashes at her stomach, and then pulled her skirt back over her legs, covering his work. He glanced both ways up and down the street and saw it was still empty. He wiped his hands on the rag the knife had been wrapped in then used it to rewrap the knife.

Taking a last look around, he walked away from the body onto Brady Street, tucking the bloody rag into his inner jacket pocket as he went. Ahead of him was Whitechapel Road. He could see the roof of the Royal London Hospital as he made his way to Bedford Street, keeping his head low and his bloody hands in his pockets. If anyone should question him about the blood he would tell them where he worked. What he did. A surgeon's assistant with blood on them was not at all unusual. It was perfect. A wave of euphoria overcame him as this time, he was sure that his work would be noticed. He had left her in a place she could not be ignored. The way he had cut her fatty flesh, the copper smell which filled his nostrils were feelings which he could not wait to feel again.

Next time, the whore will be spread all over, the rancid insides left out to air

Eventually, he arrived at his lodgings on Jane Street. It was almost four in the morning, yet he was not tired. He washed the blood from his hands, elated and charged with an excitement and energy which he had never experienced before. Clean and with a change of clothes, he fell into the chair by the fire and closed his eyes.

Soon, whores, you will bleed like the animals you are. Until then, fear will keep you until I come. You *will all feel my wrath.*

Still unable to sleep, he paced the empty rooms of his lodgings, watching as the sky faded from black to grey, signalling the new day. He wondered if they had found her yet and if they had what they had made of his work. He wanted to see, to feel the fear on the streets, to hear the speculation. He could wait no longer. Edward pulled on his coat and left the house.

He arrived at Buck's Row, to find a scene very

different to the one he had left earlier. A huge crowd of people had gathered and were being ushered back by police officers. This was what he had wanted. The Drama, the uproar, He shoved his way through to the front, desperate to see the body in the full light of day, but all he could see was a flash of green dress material and a pale leg.

'What happened?' he asked a man beside him in the crowd.

'Somebody offed a whore. Slit her throat by the looks of it,'

'Here in the street?'

'Aye, I walked past not fifteen minutes before they found her and didn't see a thing.'

Lucky me.

Edward retreated across the street. He watched the growing crowd as they speculated on who might be responsible for such a bold murder and felt a surge of elation second only to the act itself. There was an excitement in the air. He watched as people flashed each other nervous glances, or spoke in animated huddles of threes and fours.

He was proud of his achievement and imagined it was how a new father would feel at the birth of a child. Satisfied, he walked away from the crowd, occasionally looking over his shoulder to check on his handiwork. He was determined that next time he would give the crowds more to talk about. He would cut the next one deeper, make more of a show. The conflict that had been within him had gone, and now only the thirst to do his work remained.

CHAPTER FIFTEEN

Hapgood cleared his throat and stared at Miller. 'Something wrong?'

'You speak of these atrocities with such indifference. It is difficult to hear.'

'Do not waste your time thinking of the whores. They received only what they deserved and are long in their graves in any case.'

'They did not deserve to die in such a gruesome manner, no matter the circumstances of their lives.'

'And what would be the alternative? To allow them to parade their filthy flesh and pass on their disease to anyone with a few pennies to spare? No. Their fate was as they deserved. Justice was done.'

'I fail to see the justice in this situation. Perhaps some might say death would be a just end for you.'

'As I told you in the kitchen, death holds no fear

for me. Besides, no hangman will slip his noose on me, I can assure you. You may not agree with me and that is your right.'

Hapgood tossed his pen aside. 'Perhaps I no longer wish to hear of it. There is only so much horror a man can take.'

'Perhaps not.' Miller agreed 'I could leave you this night, Hapgood. Give you your peace and leave you to consider if you wish to hear the rest.' Miller looked at him, a wry smile appearing on his lips. 'Perhaps I could come back at a later date when your wife is home. How I would love to meet her.'

The threat was obvious, not so much in Miller's voice, but in his eyes. Hapgood noticed they had taken on a predatory, vacant look which Hapgood suspected was the one Miller used back in his prime, back when he was a dangerous animal. It had never occurred to him that the beast could still be there. Controlled yes, but there all the same. 'No, we shall finish tonight, if only so I can be rid of you and your evil from my home.' Hapgood grunted.

'You are just like the rest. Quick to judge

without knowing the facts. You with your perfect life which has never known the meaning of struggle and has never been forced through hardship such as I.'

'People suffer hardship every day without resorting to butchering women.'

Miller turned to look at the fire, fists clenched in his lap. 'Perhaps we should continue on before one of us does something the other may regret. We have but scratched the surface of what is yet to be told.'

'Yes, perhaps we should,' Hapgood said, agreeing that diffusing the situation was the best option. He took a fresh piece of paper and prepared to write.

'So September began with the infamy I desired. Whitechapel was rife with talk of the whore's death. For the next few nights, I wondered the streets, listening to the chatter or the drunken conversations in the pubs about my work. It was a few days into September on a cold damp evening when I was to encounter a man who would become both a thorn in my side and a catalyst for my continued efforts to shock and scare the people of England.

CHAPTER SIXTEEN

It was a little after midnight, and Bucks Row was silent. Interest in the Nichols murder had waned and no evidence remained of what had transpired just a few nights before. Edward stood at the spot, looking at the ground where the whore had bled to death. He looked for any trace of his work, but the blood had long been washed away. It already felt like such a long time ago, and the heat of rage was building up inside him again. He took his cigarettes from his pocket and started to search his pockets, looking for his matches.

From behind came the sound of a match being struck. He spun around startled to see the shadowy figure of a man across the street, the orange glow of his cigarette glowing in the darkness. The figure approached Edward, the shadows bleeding away as he stepped into the moonlight.

'Need a light?' the man asked, handing the matches to Edward.

'Thank you,' Edward said as he took the matches and lit his cigarette. The man from the shadows was well dressed, wearing a brown suit with a white shirt and tie. His face was puffy, and he had large sideburns which came down low and formed a moustache. Atop his head, he wore a bowler hat. The man's eyes were sharp and watched Edward with intense curiosity.

His cigarette lit, Edward handed the matches back to the man. 'Thank you.'

The man nodded and looked beyond Edward the pavement. 'Nasty business here the other night.'

'Yes, I heard all about it.'

'I suspect everyone in Whitechapel has by now. I wonder though what brings you out here at such a late hour.'

'I suppose I wanted to see for myself. Curiosity, perhaps.'

'Indeed. Most in this area I believe visited on the morning of the murder.'

'I hear there was quite the crowd,' Edward said

The man took a long drag on his cigarette. 'Could I have your name, Sir?' he asked as he exhaled a plume of smoke.

'Only if I can have yours first.'

'I am Inspector Abberline. I'm the officer in charge of this investigation.' The man said, holding out a hand to Edward.

'Apologies inspector, I did not know you were with the police,' Edward replied as he shook Abberline's hand, his gut contracting in fear at the unexpected turn of events.

'Indeed. And now sir if I could have your name now you have mine?'

'Miller... James Miller.'

Edward didn't know why he had given his father's name. His mind was more often doing things of its own accord without his input.

'Do you live in the area, Mr Miller?'

'Fenton Street,' he replied, again lying. He lived

on Jane Street but had bloody clothing and his knife in his lodgings and wasn't prepared to give his real address until he had moved them.

'Jane Street,' repeated Abberline. 'And where were you on the night of the murder, Mr Miller?'

'I was at home, Inspector, sleeping as any respectable man would at that hour. Surely I am not under suspicion for this terrible crime?'

'Everyone is a suspect until the killer is caught. Anyone who walks the streets and lingers at the murder site is bound to be asked questions.'

'I would hardly call it lingering. I just wanted to see the scene. Surely that is no crime.'

'No, it is not. Even so, perhaps you should move along and pursue something less morbid.'

'Yes, perhaps I should. Thank you, Inspector, for the match.'

Miller walked away from Abberline, a mixture of fury and fear within him. Although he didn't look back he could feel the Inspector watching him. He needed a drink if only to calm his nerves and made his way to the Ten Bells, which as always was crowded and noisy. He pushed his way through to the bar and waited to be served as he looked for an empty corner to hide away in. He was about to give up when he saw Mary at one of the small tables in the corner. Edward shoved his way through the crowd towards her.

'Mary?'

'Oh, Mr Miller, how are you?'

'May I join you?'

'I'm afraid I'm not good company today, but please, take a seat.'

Miller sat opposite her, mesmerised by how beautiful she was. He had to remind himself she was a filthy whore just like the others, although the conflict within him had returned at seeing her likeness to Lucy.

'I heard the news about your friend, I'm sorry for your loss,' He said as he pushed the rage aside.

'Thank you. It was a shock, I have known Polly ever since I moved to Whitechapel.'

Miller nodded and sipped his drink. 'The streets are dangerous. You might be best to stay off them until this man is caught.'

'If only I had that choice. My lodgings won't pay for themselves I'm afraid, and I must do what is necessary to keep going.'

'Is there no other way?' He asked, feeling the old sting of jealousy at the thought of a man being with her.

'I wish there were. All I have is my body which I am forced to sell for money.'

'Surely someone so attractive would have no trouble finding a nice man to settle with.'

Her smile made him ache inside and drew attention to his loneliness. 'Are you offering, Mr Miller?'

He wanted very much to say yes, yet the pain of his experience with Lucy and the things she had done, the things his mother had done made it impossible. In addition, there was his work, his beautiful work that had just begun and was nowhere close to ending. She was waiting for an answer, and Edward had no choice but to give her one. 'I believe you can find a much better man than me.'

'You have a poor opinion of yourself. You are a good looking gent if you don't mind me saying so.'

'I'm afraid my work is quite time-consuming at the moment, and I could not give you the life you deserve.'

'What do you do as a job?'

'I work in the hospital, nothing as extravagant as a doctor, I'm simply a porter.'

'You are lucky to have work at all. It's hard out there.'

They were silent for a moment, Mary swilling the last dregs of drink in her glass as he watched her. He was wondering what would be more beautiful, to see her milky flesh naked and calling to him, or flayed open to the bone.

'Would you like another drink?' he asked.

'No, I'm not feeling too well tonight, I just like to have a couple before I head out to work. It makes it easier to tolerate.'

'Do you not fear that Polly's killer will strike again?' It was the dark thing within him that had asked the question. He could feel it lingering in his mind, waiting to strike.

'Of course, but what choice do I have?'

'I'm sorry; I didn't mean to cause offence.'

'It's ok, I'm not upset, I just wish there was another way I could...' She finished her drink and stood. 'I have to go Mr Miller. I have work to do.'

'Won't you stay for another drink?'

'I can't, I have to go. Thank you for talking to me tonight.'

Without waiting for his reply, she left. He stayed for another few hours and drank. Later that night he staggered home filled with a great and dark depression. He arrived at his lodgings, fell into bed and lapsed into a sleep filled with dreams of blood and flayed flesh then woke at first light, biting his hand to stifle the screams brought on by his nightmare and wondering if he was starting to lose his grip on sanity.

For the next three days, he did not leave the house. Instead, he walked from room to room, lost in his own thoughts. He had no appetite and found sleep hard to come by that wasn't plagued with nightmares. His mood was only lightened by thoughts of Mary, and yet whenever she came to his mind, the dark thing spoke, whispering to him from the shadows.

You know what you have to do. Make the streets run red with the blood of another whore

He tried to push his thoughts aside. It was too soon after the last and Abberline made him nervous. He was sure the Inspector had seen through his deception, and at every sound expected him to burst through the door and make an arrest.

His eyes drifted to the locked cabinet which contained his knife, cleaned and sharpened since his last outing. Just a week had passed since the first whore and yet he knew he must strike again if only to silence the dark thing in his mind. He decided that he would leave it to fate. If he found sleep that night, he would strike the very next.

CHAPTER SEVENTEEN

The evening of September eighth was cool and overcast, and somewhat refreshed following an undisturbed night's sleep, Edward felt strong and ready to continue his work. He walked the streets, watching the world go by. The whores were abundant in number and swarming on every other street corner or doorway, watching him with their greedy eyes. He tried to ignore them, yet found his gaze drawn time and time again towards them, all shapes and sizes, all ages. He looked up to see a group of four boys heading in the opposite direction. They were drunk and locked eyes on him as they drew near. A bristle of excitement and discomfort surged through him, and he lowered his gaze, hoping to pass them without incident. One of the boys nudged his shoulder as they passed.

'You fuckin' watch where you walk,'

He fought the urge to confront them, not wanting to draw undue attention to himself. Already they were attracting a few glances from the multitudes of houses and doorways that lined the street.

'Oi, are you fuckin' deaf? I'm talking to you, cunt.' The boy said.

Edward walked on, trying not to react.

'You keep walking, or I might decide to cut you. We own these streets.'

Edward stopped. And turned to look at the boy. He was around seventeen, his blonde hair matted and sat on his head in a nondescript clump. His face was filthy and covered with spots, and his ratty eyes darted as he stood in the centre of the street, chest out and shoulders back, his three friends standing behind him and not looking quite as confident as their leader.

Edward walked towards the boy, who showed a flicker of surprise.

'We got a brave one ere' lads'

Edward came to a stop around a foot in front of

the boy, looking him up and down. Adrenaline surged through him, as he fought to keep his composure. 'Maybe you boys should walk away, you wouldn't want to start something you can't finish,' Edward said.

'You want me to cut you?' The boy said pulling out a small knife. Edward looked at it, then to the boy, and laughed. He saw a flash of uncertainty and fear go through the boy's face before it was swamped by his bravado.

Edward reached into his pocket and pulled out his own knife which was much larger and sharper.

The boy was afraid, but not enough to back down in front of his friends. 'Who do you think you are? Ill fuckin' cut you, mark my words.' He said, the confidence draining from him.

Edward smiled, leaning close. Underneath the filth and alcohol, he could smell the fear.

'I'm the Whitechapel killer,' he whispered. 'And unless you want to be next, I suggest you move along.'

The boy opened his mouth as if to say something

then closed it again. After a few seconds, he put away his knife. 'You ain't worth my time anyway,' he mumbled, as he turned and walked away, swiftly followed by his friends who looked more than a little confused. Edward heard the church at Spitalfields chime for two in the morning and was surprised at how much time had passed since he had set out earlier that evening. A bitter disappointment overcame him that he would not complete his work that night, which was quickly followed by an overwhelming desire to drink, something which had become more and more dominant in his life of late. He started to head towards the Ten Bells and then paused. In his current mood, he did not want to risk running into Mary and decided instead to drink in the Britannia, which was just a few minutes away on Commercial Street.

CHAPTER EIGHTEEN

The sky was beginning to lighten and the first rays of the new day were pushing away the night by the time he started to stagger home. He needed to urinate and knew it would not wait until he made it home. He looked at the homes around him and knew these were shared, sometimes with up to ten different lodgings housed inside each of the three-floor buildings. Ahead of him, the door to Twenty Nine Hanbury Street opened and a man exited, walking past him, eyes down as he hurried up the street. Edward grabbed the door before it had time to close and slipped inside. He moved down the short corridor and opened the back door, intending to use the outhouse. As he stepped out he froze, his heart racing as he almost knocked the woman down who was on the other side of the door.

'Watch it,' she said to him, stepping back in anger. Her expression then changed as she flashed him a smile. 'You almost knocked me down then my love,' she whispered.

She was a whore. Edward could tell and was of no doubt the man he saw exit the house just moments before had been a customer.

'Do you want the business then?' she asked.

'Here?' Edward replied as his inner monologue questioned the decision

Too risky. It's almost daylight and look at all these windows. Somebody is bound to see you.

'I come here all the time. As long as we keep quiet, it will be fine.' She encouraged, taking a step closer to him as he stood in the doorway.

Don't do it, you'll get us caught. The whore's blood will spill another day

With a nod of the head, he stepped into the yard, allowing the door to close behind him.

'That's it. Come on love. Come to Annie. Up against the fence will do it.' she said.

Windows overlooked the yard from the house

itself and the houses next door and across the street. The chances of being disturbed were high, and yet he was unable to stop himself. The whore was leaning against the fence, waiting for him.

'Let me just pull this up. You get the old fella ready,' she said as she grabbed her skirts.

'Wait,' he whispered to her in the dark.

'What is it, love?' she asked.

'Are you sure you want to do this Mary?'

'Who the bleedin' ell is Mary?' she asked, a confused look etched onto her round face.

'For an extra tuppence, it's yours,' he snarled.

'Whatever suits you love. Come on then. Come to Mary.'

He approached as she hitched up her skirts. He could smell her, unwashed and filthy and imagined he could feel his skin recoil in disgust.

'Come on then, get it out. Give him to Mary to look after,' she panted, reaching for his crotch.

'What's wrong with it? It's not getting hard.' She looked at him and froze, realising too late the danger she was in.

'No, murder,' she said as his fingers latched onto her windpipe and shoved her back, her head slamming against the fence. He squeezed, watching her eyes, first filled with fear, then with glassy and expressionless disinterest. He lowered her to the floor, astounded that they had not yet been disturbed. The sky was now a light grey in colour, the cover of darkness almost gone. He went through her pockets taking out her belongings and arranging them at her feet in the same way he would prepare instruments for the doctors in the hospital. This time, though, it was his work and his patient. He was the surgeon. He took her hand and with some effort removed the two brass rings on her fingers, before slipping them into his pocket.

What are you doing? There is not the time for this.

He ignored the voice in his head, and took his knife from his pocket, believing God would protect him until he completed his work.

CHAPTER NINETEEN

Later.

Abberline crouched by the body, his nose wrinkling as he looked at the mess.

'Godley, come here,' he said over his shoulder.

'Yes, Sir?'

'He's left this one a right mess. All these people watching isn't helping.'

'I know sir. They don't miss a trick around here. Some of them are charging to let people in to view the body from the upstairs windows.'

'Animals,' Abberline muttered

'What do you make of that, Sir?' Godley asked, pointing to the feet of the body where her belongings had been carefully arranged. Abberline frowned, standing from his crouched position.

'I'm not sure. I'm sure it meant something to him.'

Godley looked at the body, absently rubbing the edges of his moustache.

'He really cut her up didn't he, Boss. You think it's the same fella who did the other one?'

'That's the one thing I'm certain of. This was done by the same... hand.'

Abberline crouched by the body again,

'What is it, boss?' Godley said.

'Rings. He took her rings. You can see the marks where they were. Thereon her fingers. Two of them. Cheap brass has stained the skin. See?' Abberline stood and flicked a sour glare at the windows and those who looked down on the scene.

'The public will have a field day with this,' Godley said, shaking his head.

'I get the impression that's what he wants. Our killer is a showman.'

'What do you mean, Sir?'

'Just look at her, Godley. The way he's positioned the innards over her shoulder, how he's left this one open and exposed. The first one was covered up. This entire scene has been set up to be noticed. He likes the attention.'

'I don't know about that, but he certainly took a risk. A witness from inside says he was out here sitting on the back step fixing a boot at around quarter to five. He didn't see a thing.'

'Quarter to five? That means that our killer did this in almost full daylight.'

'A risk, especially as you say, with all these windows overlooking the yard.'

'I count twenty windows where someone could have seen our killer not to mention footfall from the building. Whores are known to use this yard to do their business.'

'Surely that's good, Sir.'

'What do you mean?'

'It means he's sloppy.'

'It means he's dangerous, Godley.' Abberline looked at the faces pressed to the windows surrounding the yard. 'Get statements from everyone, and I mean everyone. Don't be afraid to lean on them if you have to. People around here will be reluctant to talk to us. Tell them if they don't talk to you then they can deal with me. They know me around here and are aware I won't stand for it.'

'What about the press?'

'No point keeping it back with all these witnesses looking at the scene. Prepare a statement.'

'Yes, sir.'

'But Godley?'

'Yes, sir?'

'Don't mention the rings. Hold that back. You can tell them the rest. I want something only he had I will know if we get someone for this.'

'Yes sir,' said Godley, before heading back into the house. Abberline looked at the body, his eyes drifting to the entrails which lay in a soggy heap by the woman's head. Edward watched from the upper window of the next door house, looking down from above at his handiwork. He listened to the excited chatter of the people around him. There was a nervous tension in the air and with each speculative statement about the kind of monster that could be responsible, he found that he grew more and more satisfied with his night's work.

She was as he had left her, however, he noticed that she looked altogether more glorious in daylight. He regarded his work, the way the stomach cavity lay open and exposed, the whore's stomach piled up next to her face. He couldn't wait until they found out he had taken some away with him, some of the insides of the whore which he had fed to a few mangy street dogs on his way home. He wondered what Abberline would make of that. He had enjoyed this one more than the first. The risk of how easily he could have been caught was worth it if only for the thrill it had given him. He recalled how her flesh tore, how steam rose from the body cavity in the cool early morning air. Amid the chaos that surrounded him, he was at peace.

And what about the next one, how will you shock the people more than this?

It was a good question and one that deserved some thought. Perhaps he could deliver some to the police, send them a part of the next whore. Edward looked at the inspector, who was now in deep conversation with a doctor. Edward recognised him from the hospital but didn't know his name.

He was suddenly too warm and uncomfortable and wanted some fresh air and

A drink?

He was concerned that he was becoming dependent on alcohol, and needed to keep that aspect in control. His father had been a heavy drinker, and Edward wondered if that particular trait had been passed on to him. He shoved his way through the crowd, his prime place at the window swallowed by someone else the second he had moved. Edward went outside and leaned on the wall, feeling giddy and light-headed.

He saw the officer who was speaking to Abberline in the yard approach him.

'Are you alright, Sir?'

Edward nodded. 'Yes, it's just... it was a horrific sight.'

'Indeed, it is, sir. Then again you made the decision to pay to see it.'

Edward swallowed his rage. 'I was curious. As you can see I'm not alone in that regard.'

Godley looked him up and down then took out his notepad. 'I wonder if you might answer a few questions?'

'I am unsure how I can help, but of course, I will assist in any way I can.'

'May I ask what time you arrived here at the scene?'

'Oh, it was perhaps twenty minutes ago.'

'Did you see anything unusual on your way here, Mr....'

'Miller, Edward Miller. And no, I'm sorry, I did not see anything at all untoward. There was already quite a crowd when I arrived.'

Godley spoke again, but Edward didn't hear him, he was looking over the detective's shoulder to where Abberline stood watching.

'Mr. Miller?'

'I'm sorry, could you say that again?'

Godley opened his mouth to speak again when Abberline spoke first. 'Godley, could I have a word please?'

Godley glanced to Abberline, nodded

acknowledgement, then turned back to Miller. 'Wait here Mr Miller, I'll be back in just a moment.'

Godley jogged over the inspector, leaving Edward alone with his thoughts. He wanted to run but knew that would mean the game was up. Like it or not he would have to play this out. He could see Abberline watching him as he spoke to Godley, those cold eyes always calculating, always working things out.

Careful with this one, he's not like the others

Edward was afraid of Abberline. He wanted to tear out those calculating eyes and be left alone to do his work. He watched them now in conversation, sure Abberline was asking why the same man had shown up at consecutive crime scenes. Edward waited for Godley to return.

'Apologies, Mr Miller. The inspector has asked me to collect statements from all who were present. I wonder if you would be so kind as to come to the station this afternoon and answer a few questions.'

Miller nodded, feeling Abberline's gaze burning into the back of his skull. 'I'm not sure how much I can tell you, however, I will assist in any way I can.'

'Excellent Mr Miller. We appreciate your cooperation.'

Godley nodded then returned to the inspector as Miller made his way home, unsure how the situation had just unfolded and how it was going to end.

CHAPTER TWENTY

Hapgood looked at Miller, who was coughing again. He wiped the blood from his mouth and stuffed the handkerchief in his pocket.

'They had you? They actually had you there at the scene of the crime?' Hapgood said. 'Surely you didn't go.'

'How could I not? To not attend would be the same as admitting guilt. Of course, the fool Godley did not concern me, he was as gullible and stupid as the rest, but Abberline… he was different.'

'You sound almost respectful of him.'

'Of course. He was my nemesis. How is the good Inspector these days? I hope he is keeping well?'

'He is keeping well. We speak regularly about his Memoirs. He often visits me to check on their progress.' Hapgood said.

Miller nodded, his expression hard to read. 'I often wish the inspector and I could sit and discuss the way our paths had become entwined. It would make for an interesting conversation, would it not? In some ways, I looked up to him, even back then. I saw Abberline as the man I could have been had circumstances been different. Perhaps one day, he will read your book, Hapgood.'

'Having known Fred for some time I fail to see any similarities between you.'

'Of course not, for you are just an ordinary man. The inspector and I are two of a kind. His good to my evil, the light to my darkness. You are a writer,

Are you not Hapgood? In all great fables is there not a protagonist for both good and evil?'

'I understand that, but this is not a work of fiction.'

'Of course, it isn't, however, the rules are the same. In any great story, there is an opposing force of good and evil. You need to look no further than the bible to see such an example.'

'The Bible?' repeated Hapgood. 'Are you a religious man?'

Miller considered for a moment. 'The answer is not as simple as yes or no. If you are asking if I believe in heaven and hell, then I would say no. If you are asking if there is a higher power beyond that which we know which would fit with the notion of God, then yes. Without his help, I would have surely been stopped.'

'Are you saying that your...*work* was completed with the help of God?'

Miller smiled, leaning forward so that his face was half cast in shadow.

'Of course, it was, Hapgood. All the evidence

points to the fact.'

'Would you care to elaborate?'

'Look back on all that we have discussed so far. I was a reckless man out to shock the public, I struck in near daylight with little to no caution. If the will of God was that I should stop then why did he not allow one of the whores to escape, or ensure that someone would catch me in the act? No Hapgood, to me it is clear. I was protected by a higher power.'

'Or you had incredible good fortune.'

'Are they not the same thing? Is luck not the will of God?'

'Based on the things you have said so far there was no such belief after the murder at Hanbury Street when the police were closing in on you.'

'And yet here I am.'

'Here you are,' Hapgood repeated.

Miller grinned and made himself comfortable. 'If you are ready, I shall tell you about my visit to the police station that afternoon and all that came after.'

Hapgood stretched and prepared new paper. 'I am as ready as I will be.'

'Then I shall proceed.'

Miller closed his eyes and rolled back the years, pulling the memories from the place he kept them. 'I remember the police station smelled of wood and polish. That was the one time I think I saw Abberline anything other than confident when I walked in to give my statement. Soon enough, the fragile sense of peace would be broken and our game would soon begin. First, though, I spoke to Godley at the front desk...

CHAPTER TWENTY ONE

The police station was less busy that Miller had expected. He had informed Godley of his arrival and was waiting to be seen by Abberline and had spent the morning preparing himself for any questions the Inspector may have.

'Mr Miller,' Godley said, approaching him where he waited.

'Yes?'

'The Inspector will see you now. This way please, Sir.'

Miller followed Godley behind the counter and down a short wood-panelled corridor. The monster inside him told him to run, and that he was being led into a trap. Miller ignored it, pushing it to the back of his mind as he was led into a modest office. Behind the desk, Abberline was writing a report. Godley motioned for Miller to sit then stood by the door. Miller complied, waiting for Abberline to finish writing. Abberline completed his report, then set the pen back into the inkwell.

'Mr Miller, thank you for coming.'

'As I said, inspector, I am happy to assist in any way I can.'

'As I'm sure you are aware, there is much talk on the streets about these murders. People are getting restless and demanding a response. It is my job to give it to them.'

'We rely on people like yourself to keep us safe, Inspector. People are frightened.'

'And so they should be. Nasty business this.'

Miller fidgeted, folding his hands in his lap. 'So, how can I help you?'

'Just a few questions if I may.'

Miller glanced over at Godley who was standing by the closed office door. 'I'm not sure how I can assist. I know nothing other than what I have seen in the newspapers.'

'Routine, Mr Miller. You were at both of the murder sites.'

'As were many others I'm sure. They caused quite an uproar.'

'They did indeed. And you are right, there are other people who were observed who have also been asked to come in to see me. Nothing to cause alarm, I assure you.'

'So how can I help?'

'Do you work, Mr Miller?'

'Yes, Inspector. At the hospital.'

'So you're a doctor.'

'No, sir. I'm not that skilled I'm afraid. I assist. Cleaning the operating areas, taking the dead to the morgue. Things of that nature.'

'But you do work alongside doctors? You are able to observe how they work in regards to how they operate?'

Miller suspected what Abberline was hinting at. His own words wouldn't come, lost in a melting pot of excuses. It was at this point that the black thing that lived inside him took over and answered on his behalf.

'I wouldn't say I was able to observe as such, Inspector. True enough I am present when the doctors are performing their surgeries but I do not get in the way of their work. I bring clean cloths and remove dirty ones. I clean blood when I am told to do so. Why do you ask?'

Abberline stared at him, eyes searching into his soul. It would have been enough to break Miller under normal circumstances, but the thing that was in control of him stared right back, gaze unwavering.

'We have a theory,' Abberline said, finally breaking eye contact. 'An idea that our killer could be a doctor, someone with anatomical knowledge.'

'From what I saw, Sir, he butchered those poor women. I saw no evidence of skill.'

'As I stated, it is just theory. There is another which is that our killer may work in a slaughterhouse or something similar.'

'It sounds like you don't know much if you excuse me for saying so.' Miller somehow managed not to smile when he said it.

'No, sadly we don't, which is why we are questioning as many potential witnesses as possible.'

'As I stated to you yesterday, Inspector, I know nothing that can help you. I didn't witness anything.'

'Oh, I don't know about that. You were at both murder scenes, perhaps you saw someone acting suspiciously?'

Miller shook his head. Grateful that the beast was in control. 'No, sadly not. I must admit it was my own morbid curiosity that led me to visit the areas of the murders. It isn't often such horrors are seen.'

'Even for you, Mr Miller, a man who works closely alongside surgeons. I would think you have seen more than your share of blood and violence.'

'Are you suggesting I had something to do with these murders?' He was surprised how calm the words came. Inside, the real him was screaming.

Abberline stared, the smallest hint of a smile on his lips. 'No, Mr Miller. I don't think you are capable of such terrible things. What we are looking for is a monster, and you are clearly not that.'

Miller remained motionless, even as the demon inside him screamed in rage at the dismissive attitude of Abberline. 'That's a relief. I did wonder why you asked me here.'

'Merely to gather information, Mr Miller. Nothing more.'

'Then I'm free to go?'

'Of course. If I could offer you a parting word of advice. Perhaps it would be unwise to continue visiting the scenes of these awful murders should any more take place.'

'With luck, you will catch him before that becomes an issue.'

'We intend to do just that. Even so....'

'No, I will stay away, inspector. I do not wish to impede your investigation.'

'Good. In that case, there should be no need for us to ever see each other again. Godley will show you out. Goodbye, Mr Miller.'

Miller allowed Godley to show him out, somehow keeping control of the fury that raged within him. Abberline's offhanded dismissal of his ability to conduct the crimes was burning deep, and he had already made the decision to prove them wrong. After he was shown out, Miller walked, letting the fury simmer as he mingled with the destitute and the wretched. It was clear to him that he needed to do something new to shock them and to let him know how serious he was. It was then the dark thing in his mind spoke to him. It told him that if one whore savaged and left for all to see wasn't enough, then perhaps he should do two in a single night.

Hapgood set his pen down. 'The double event. Widely reported as the boldest of the murders. Both occurring within minutes of each other.'

Miller nodded but gave no reply.

'You're saying Abberline triggered this?'

'I had to prove a point. His words were a personal insult.'

'You acted, even at the risk of being caught?'

'Capture wasn't a consideration. Understand, Hapgood, that back then, this demon beast inside me had full control over my actions. Over the years I have learned to tame it, although it still lives there, whispering in the night.'

The comment was enough to bring a moment of silence to the room. Both men contemplated as the fire crackled in the fireplace.

'So you acted on it based on your anger at

Abberline?'

'Not immediately. Even enraged I was cautious. I knew the police investigation was at its height and there were many patrols in the streets, for all the good it would do.'

'I don't understand.'

'I wonder, Hapgood, have you, as part of your research frequented Whitechapel? Have you explored its streets after dark?'

'No, I'm afraid I haven't.'

'I thought not. People without the need wouldn't frequent such squalid areas.'

'I have been there, of course, but not at night. I did wonder how you could so easily avoid detection.'

'It was different then, Hapgood. There were none of the lamps on the streets that are there today. At night, Whitechapel was a maze of shadows and filth. If you remained quiet and still, you could stand a few feet from a passing police patrol and they would never see you. Even so, the public was on alert, and so I decided it was best if I delayed my work until a later date.'

'And what did you do to fill the gap?'

Miller shifted in his seat, uncomfortable at the line of questioning. Hapgood noticed his discomfort.

'You don't have to tell me of course. I was under the impression that you wished to give a full account of your story.'

'Fear not. I will tell it as it happened, I am simply organising my thoughts. In order to keep that demon inside me at bay, I acquired some opiates from the hospital. I took these in combination with drinking in an effort to keep my demon from taking control. That, Hapgood, was perhaps the darkest period of my younger years. Alone in my lodgings listening to that thing whisper in my mind or drinking away the pain in some hovel amid the vile creatures I had vowed to destroy. It was during one of those drunken stupors that my path was shaped. It was the end of September, the twenty eighth as I recall when I lost control to the demon and two days later would commit what you refer to as the double event. By that time, of course, I had the name I would become known by.'

'Yes. The letter you sent to the police. You gave yourself the name Jack the Ripper.'

Miller smiled, the expression coming as more of a grimace. 'That name had nothing to do with me, Hapgood, I can assure you. I wrote no letters to the police.'

Hapgood stared at Miller as the rain probed the windows for a way in. 'I don't understand. Everyone knew you as the Ripper. Even Inspector Abberline thought you were responsible for at least some of the letters sent under that name.'

'Newspapers, Hapgood. Those ghouls lived for stories such as mine. Murder in the streets, the police unable to catch a killer. Every journalist looking for a new angle, some new information to sell more copies. Is it beyond the realm of possibility that one particularly creative individual might have forged a gruesome letter and signed it in a name guaranteed to cause public panic?'

'I never considered the possibility.'

'As I said when I arrived earlier this evening. There is much you do not know about my life. Much yet that you will still learn. Are you ready to proceed?'

Hapgood adjusted his papers and picked up his pen. 'Yes. Proceed when ready.'

Miller folded his hands in his lap then took a deep breath as he recalled the past. 'As I stated, it was the twenty eighth of September and had been another night of drinking myself into a stupor. It was as I was walking the streets that once again fate conspired to steer me in the path it had determined I should take.

CHAPTER TWENTY TWO

The sheer volume of noise in the Ten Bells was enough to block the violent whispers in Miller's mind. He had found that drinking helped, and at the same time come to two unrelated conclusions. The first was, as he sat in the corner, the belly full of drink churning and threatening to make an unwanted reappearance, that he wasn't too far removed from many of the seedy clientele surrounding him. He had always considered himself to be a step above, a higher class than the wretched and the desperate, but had come to realise that he too was wretched. He too was desperate. The second thing he had come to realise is that he was falling in love with Mary Kelly. They had met only a few times and yet whenever they did so the beast inside was silent. The conversation was easy and she was, to him beautiful. Her features delicate, skin soft.

Just like Lucy.

Miller had decided that if one thing would allow him to stop with his work, then finding love, real love with a woman who felt the same and wouldn't hurt him, could be it. He had taken to frequenting the pubs he knew she would go to, yet had only seen her two or three times. She, like the rest of the population of Whitechapel, was in fear of the Ripper, of him. He knew the beast inside found a great pleasure in listening to the whispers of fear and speculation as to when he would next strike. To sit there amid it, able to almost taste the fear, should have been intoxicating and exactly what he had hoped to achieve, yet all he could think about was Mary. He wanted to tell her how he felt, part of him sure she would feel the same way, the other half of him afraid she would reject him and shatter his fragile confidence like every other woman in his life had done.

You're supposed to want to kill them. Not fuck them.

Miller took another drink. He had grown to hate the thing that lived within him. The thing shaped by his misery and despair. It had grown into a cruel inner passenger, something which he hated as much as he needed it. He wondered if she would feel the same way if he told her how he felt. He would tell her he could take her away from the life on the streets. Give her security and safety in exchange for filling the loveless void inside him and helping him banish his demon.

What about Abberline? Remember how he said you were incapable of the work we had done? Remember how you wanted to prove him wrong?

'No.' Miller slurred. Nobody heard it due to the volume of noise around him. Usually, drink worked, but today the beast was strong and it went on, poison tongue moving as it spoke to him.

I thought you wanted to be special. I thought you wanted to be remembered? Do you really think falling in love with a whore is going to give you that fame?

'Shut up.'

Just listen. It's everywhere. Everyone is talking about us and our work. I know you're trying to drink me away, but you don't fool me. You thrive on this. Somebody actually knowing who you are. Our work is good. We need to continue. Kill the whores like you said you would.

'Stop talking to me.'

'Mr Miller?'

'Mary, hello…' Miller looked away. He hated her seeing him like this. Broken and vulnerable, a drunk wrestling with his inner demons. 'I didn't expect to see you here.'

The statement, he knew, was stupid. He had been frequenting the places he knew she would be in the hope of seeing her. Now he was the worse for drink, he just wanted to be alone. Instead of leaving, Mary sat opposite him. Miller straightened in his seat, trying as best he could to convince her he was lucid.

'Drinking alone?' her eyes fell to the empty glass on the table.

'Yes, I suppose I am. Would you like to join me?'

He saw a change in her expression, a shadow of a frown. He wondered if she could see the glaze in his eyes or hear the slur in his voice. 'No, I can't stop I'm afraid. I just saw you here and wanted to say hello.'

'Are you sure you don't want a drink with me?' Miller slurred, unable to control or act in the way his rational side demanded. 'You and I could make a night of it.'

Mary shifted in her seat. 'No, I really can't. I have to go to work.'

'Work? If that is the only thing stopping you from drinking with me, then here.' Miller tossed two pennies on the table. 'How much time does that buy?' He hated saying it, despising himself as the words left his mouth, yet the dark thing was controlling him and he was a powerless passenger. The pained expression he saw on Mary's face hurt him more than he anticipated.

'I think you've had too much drink, Mr Miller.'

Miller gripped the edge of the table. Nausea and disgust at his behaviour making a nasty concoction in his stomach. 'Yes. I think you may be right.'

He lurched to his feet, the black thing inside alive and intending to make him pay for trying to repress it. He could hear it in his mind, a distant echo moving closer as it demanded blood. As he lurched to his feet, Miller nudged the table with his legs, knocking over his glass, Mary flinched away from him, clearly disturbed.

This is why you are alone. This is why we have to do our work. Delay no further. Too much time has been wasted. Let us show Abberline how capable you are.

'I'm sorry,' he slurred as he staggered towards the door. The monster inside him was close to taking full control. He could feel it growing inside, filling his veins, occupying his muscles, its oozing filth polluting his brain. He knew there was only one way to sate its thirst. One thing that would give him respite. It was demanding blood and blood it would get.

CHAPTER TWENTY THREE

'I have a question, if I may.' Hapgood said, setting his pen down and stretching his arm out in front of him. Miller looked at him his expression neutral. Taking the silence as the go ahead to ask his question, Hapgood continued. 'You speak of the thing inside you driving you to do the…things you did. It seems to me that it or you were quite ready to claim another victim there and then on the night of the twenty eighth. I was curious as to why it took place two days later instead.'

'Would you like me to answer now or give you a moment to rest your writing hand?'

'By all means answer, I will make notes before we continue.'

'Very well.' Miller said. He watched as Hapgood stood and walked towards the window, stretching his arms and trying to banish the stiffness which was setting in on his muscles. Hapgood looked out at the wet and deserted streets and realised he no longer had any desire to escape. He wanted to hear more. He glanced at Miller who, to his surprise was staring at him.

'Would you like another drink, Mr Miller?'

Miller shook his head. 'No, thank you. Fortunately, the man I am now has more control over his habits than the one we have been discussing. That, in part, is the answer to your question, Hapgood. That night, as I left the Ten Bells, the thing inside was enraged, ready to spill the blood of any whore in its path and the intention was to do just that. I recall little in the way of detail due to the ferocity of the rage. I remember making for my lodgings, anticipating collecting my knife and adding to my tally. Sadly, my drink addled body was incapable. I recall reaching my home and heading inside then my next recollection was when daylight had broken and I woke on the floor with my previous evening's consummation in great pools around me.'

'The drink stopped you.'

'Yes. It appears so. Perhaps it was for the best. I was in no condition to complete the task I had set myself.'

Hapgood returned to his seat. He was exhausted by the sheer volume of knowledge he had taken in. 'Alcohol it seems was a constant in your existence.'

'Indeed it was. I had developed an uncontrollable shake of the right hand which would only be stilled by more consumption.'

'You had become addicted.'

'Yes. And I was aware that the consequences of the drink rendered me powerless to do my work. As fate would have it, the very thing that I detested, the dark part of my psyche that was desperate to gain full control over me was more powerful than the need for drink, and so that day, it made me suffer the pain and ignore the craving as it had desires of it's own to attend to. It was later, before midnight that my hand was still enough to conduct my work, and with Inspector Abberline's words fresh in my mind, I set out to once again strike fear into the streets.

CHAPTER TWENTY FOUR

Miller walked the filthy cobbles, enduring the steady rain which fell without respite. He was colder still inside, though and thought only of his task ahead as he passed anonymous faces in the night, cap pulled low over his eyes. Despite the killings and the hysteria in the news, it seemed the destitute still filled the streets, and the whores still went about their business and took their customers to dark and secluded areas where their bodily transactions could be completed. He walked without aim. Assessing opportunities. He desperately wanted to stop at the Ten Bells and apologise to Mary, but he dare not see her with the thing inside him in control. It was the one guiding his actions and its need for blood would not be denied. For Miller, it had become an external experience. He felt like he was detached somehow from himself and that he was merely observing the events unfold. Certainly, there was a sense of excitement and anticipation. The thing inside him reminded Miller that this was what he wanted. It reminded him of his mother, and of Lucy. He passed a patrolling policeman, the oil lamp he was carrying hardly strong enough to puncture the deep black shadows at every turn. The thing inside reminded him of Abberline and what he had said. It was this which reminded him to allow the monster inside him to take control. He had been scouring the streets for more than two hours in the search of a perfect opportunity, each passing moment the fury within him growing to something he knew he would not be able to control. He had already chosen his victim and was awaiting his opportunity to strike. There was no reason he knew of why he had chosen her. Something about her look had drawn him. He wondered again if there was some unknown connection to his mother or Lucy which was controlling his selections. No matter, he had decided that this was the one he would take as soon as the opportunity arose. He followed her at a distance, watching as she tried to solicit herself to anyone who may show interest. He watched from the shadows as she stood on Berner Street talking to a man. The man grabbed her by the arm and tried to pull her into the street. Miller watched, hoping he wasn't about to lose his victim. The man then shoved the woman down onto the ground and walked away. Miller watched him go, the street deserted. The thing in his mind told him it was time to make his move. He walked out of the shadows and approached, flashing his broadest smile designed to instil trust.

'Are you alright, miss?' he said as he helped her to her feet, his eyes flicking to the open doors to Dutfield Yard at her back, the enticing opaque passage an open maw ready to receive those looking for privacy from prying eyes. She too was mostly dressed all in black, another detail which would help him keep prying eyes away from them within the dark.

'I'm fine, bloody idiot rough handled me a bit, that's all.'

Up close she was older than she first appeared. She was staring at him, trying to assess if he was a potential customer. Miller would have liked to play along but knew time was of the essence if he were to do two, and was cautious of the man she had just been arguing with and if he might come back. She took a packet of Cashew nuts from her pocket.

'Thank you for helping me up. It's rare to find nice people around here. Do you want a nut? They really are-'

He struck. Clamping one hand around her throat and the other over her mouth, he pushed her back into the pitch dark of the archway, the interior of the yard offering complete darkness. Surprised by the suddenness of his actions as he pushed her, she stumbled over her own feet, the two of them landing hard on the ground. Miller could hardly see her, and let his instinct guide him, he squeezed her throat as hard as he could, reaching into his jacket for his knife which was wrapped in rags as she clawed and scratched at him, desperate to escape. Sitting astride her, he let go and she squirmed onto her side. He struck her on the side of the head, the force making her skull hit the concrete hard enough to stun her. She stopped fighting but he could hear her wheezing, still alive but unable to call for help. Miller unwrapped the knife, the weight of it solid in his hands. He had decided to make a real mess of this one. To string the innards up over the entrance to the yard. He had decided if Abberline wanted to see what he was capable of, then that's what he would do. He put a hand over her face and pushed her head to the side, exposing her neck. He could just see it in the almost total darkness. The knife split the skin easily, the fury within him making him cut deep enough to slice through the neckerchief she was wearing. Blood which looked black in the gloom seeped out, pooling over her throat. She exhaled one last time and was silent, the nerves and arteries in her neck severed. He was preparing to start the next phase of his work when he heard a sound, an approaching horse and cart. He stopped moving, hoping it would pass and let him continue. He looked over his shoulder from where he sat astride the body, the relative light of the street ensuring all his fears were realised. The horse appeared and turned into the alleyway. Miller knew the path ahead was blocked and there was no way out. Reacting on instinct, he scrambled to his feet, startling the horse which shied away and reared back. This was it. He knew he would be caught. There was no way he could escape the alley without being seen. Slightly ahead, the yard veered off to the left into another short passage terminating in a wall. Miller turned into it, pressing himself into the brick in the hope of remaining unseen. He watched as the horse and cart entered the yard, the horse still unsettled by the presence of Miller. He only hoped the man on the cart couldn't see him too. He watched as the horse stopped by the whore, and lean over, nudging it with his whip. Miller looked on, his nerves on fire, heart thundering so loudly he was sure the man on the cart would surely hear it. The man on the cart didn't panic. He hopped down from the horse and walked towards the building adjacent to the yard. Music was spilling out of it, a club of some sort, Miller presumed. He could hear the laughter and the drunken chatter from within. It was his one chance to flee. Quickly, he walked towards the entrance to the yard, forcing himself not to rush. He exited and crossed the street, just as the man who had interrupted him returned from the club, three men with him. Miller started to walk away from the yard, unable to believe his good fortune and more convinced than ever that if there was a God, then he must be on Miller's side and agree with his work. Miller heard the man say something about a drunk asleep in the yard as he showed the men into it, then was lost in the dark, out of range to hear more. He walked quickly, the thing inside him determined to fill its promise of doing two in a single night. Miller touched his fingers to his neck, it was sore and as he pulled his fingers back, he could see blood. The whore had scratched him in her desperate fight for life and he knew if he intended to do another, he must hide the evidence of what had been done. Miller took a red handkerchief from his pocket and tied it loosely around his neck. It wasn't perfect, but it would be enough to hide the scratches. Soon, he started to encounter people rushing past him in the direction he was coming from. One man, wide eyed, stopped him as he passed.

'Have you heard? He's struck again!'

Before Miller could respond the man was on his way, desperate not to miss getting a look at the body. More people passed him, racing to the scene, and with each one, the rage grew inside him. For the first time, he and the thing that lived inside him were one, a joint force with the same goal in mind. He quickened his pace, knowing time was against him. The police would be on the way and if he were to do as he promised to show Abberline how serious he was, then he knew he must act quickly. He approached Mitre Square, the dark shadows afforded by the surrounding buildings swallowing him. As if God were presenting another opportunity to him, he saw here, waiting by the wall for business to come her way. With the dark thing in his mind on command, Miller was without the caution he would have ordinarily shown. He stalked towards her, blood pounding thick in his temples, heart beating with ferocious tempo. She saw him coming, a frown, a brief flicker of fear. He was ready to strike, and would have done so there and then had he not realised there were people close by who would see him. Miller scrambled to regain control, slowing his pace as he walked towards her. He even managed a smile in order to put her at ease.

'Apologies, I didn't intend to startle you.'

'I did wonder what you were doing, hiding in the dark.'

'Haven't you heard?'

'Heard what?'

'The Ripper. He's struck again. I saw you standing here alone and wanted to check you were safe.'

The woman grimaced, fear in her eyes. 'He's

struck again? Bloody hell, I thought that business was all over with.'

Miller looked around, noting that they were at last alone. 'Yes, it's not safe on the streets. I hear he's going to strike again.'

'You hear? And how would you know that?' The woman said, emitting a short bark of laughter.

Miller said nothing. He lunged for her, allowing the fury to take charge as he wrestled her to the ground. He cut her throat, the dim sounds of her gargling her last breath driving him on more to complete his task. He transcended then into a fury as if seeing the events through someone else's eyes. He lifted her skirts as she bled out and the knife slide into the soft flesh of her belly then rip with ease toward the breastbone. The smell of her innards, the warm coppery scent as he went about his work drove him into a frenzy as if he were a shark feeding in bait laden waters. He reached into the cavity, pulling some of the slick innards out and tossing it aside, stabbing at the rest. He looked down at her lying there, the life expired from her.

She reminded him of his mother, the way she would lay on the floor and have man after man come in and climb on top of her. The fire inside was further stoked as he hacked at her face with his blade, slicing off the nose, savaging the features so they were unrecognisable. The knife was slick now with blood and he almost lost his grip on it as he cut her in the almost near dark. He stabbed her again and again until he grunted in pain. In his frenzy and with the blood making everything slick, he had cut his own forearms he was stabbing down at her body. The pain receptors exploded in him and told him he had to go. He had ridden his fortune once tonight and had seemingly done the same a second time. He wrapped the blade in its rags and slipped them into his jacket, his hands covered in a mixture of his and the whore's blood. He couldn't tell how deeply he had cut himself and only knew the pain was intense. He clambered to his feet and walked quickly, heading away from the mess he had made and hoping to make it home without anyone seeing him. He knew he must be bloody, the whore had bled well and he suspected some of it was on him. He had a way to fix that problem at least. He crossed the street, keeping to the shadows. The people were now focused on the first kill, and all attention was diverted there. Most we removing in groups towards it, which helped him as he stuck to the shadows and kept himself out of sight. Soon enough, he saw what he was looking for. He hurried to the trough used for feeding horses. The water was cold, but it would suffice, he scooped it up, wiping his face and washing the excess blood from his hands.

'Mr Miller?'

Miller spun around, startled, spilling water down his front. For a split second, everything froze in place, there were no sounds, no smells, no euphoria at the work he had just done. Just silence. Mary was staring at him.

'Why are you drinking out of there? That's for the horses.' It was then she shifted her gaze and saw the blood on his hands. 'Why do you have blood on you?'

He couldn't answer. His brain couldn't find the words to make a viable reason as to why he was covered in blood that wasn't the truth. He was dimly aware that it was only a matter of time before she made the connection between him and the murders, and yet each passing second felt as if it had stretched for an hour. By self-preservation or by design, the black thing, still basking in the blood it had spilt, took over.

'I was attacked. Three men. One of them cut me with a knife.' Miller held out his arm and showed her the deep gash which was still weeping blood. 'I was just trying to clean it here in this trough.' He was surprised how easily the words came and how convincing they sounded. More importantly, it seemed Mary believed it too.

'That's terrible. Did they take anything from you? Money or anything?'

'Just my pride. This is quite a deep wound. I should go to the hospital I think.'

Mary shook her head. It seemed she had not yet heard the news of the murders which Miller felt was in his favour. 'No. you'll have to wait for an age for them to see you. Come with me, I live close, just over at Miller's Court. I can dress it for you to stop it bleeding at least. Then you can get to the hospital.'

'Are you sure?' Miller asked, knowing that going with Mary would be the perfect way to get off the streets amid the mass of activity that would soon fill the streets. 'I would really appreciate the assistance.'

'Of course, come on, this way.'

Mary led him away, into the warren of streets away from the violence of the work he had just committed. Miller kept his arm hidden and knew anyone who might see them together would think they were just a couple walking together, there would be no link between him and the whores he had just killed. Even the beast inside him was silent, satisfied with its night's work. It allowed Miller a clear head and some respite from its constant demands. He allowed her to lead him deeper through the streets, away from where he knew the police would be. She led him to her home, unaware of who he was, what he was capable of, and what he had done.

CHAPTER TWENTY FIVE

'It's not perfect but it's the best I could do.'

Miller looked at the makeshift bandage on his arm. He had watched as she cleaned the wound and made the covering from a man's shirt she pulled out of a drawer. 'It's good, really good. Thank you. I hope the owner of the shirt won't miss it too much.'

Mary sat on the edge of the bed, the room was tiny, no more than a box and Miller could see every detail of her skin in the light of the fire in the grate. 'No, that used to belong to Joseph.'

'You live together?' Miller asked, surprised how much the news she may be unavailable hurt him.

'Not anymore. He moved out again. We can't

seem to avoid arguing over everything.'

'I'm sorry.'

'There's nothing for you to be sorry for. It's not your fault. All I have now is this place, but even that is better than sleeping in a doss or on the streets.'

She sat beside him on the bed. In the glow of the fire, he couldn't help but be mesmerised by her beauty.

Miller knew it was time to raise the subject both of them had so far been avoiding. 'I want to apologise for my behaviour the last time we spoke. I was the worse for drink and….'

Mary shrugged. 'I've heard much worse. You should hear some of the things people say to me out on the streets. I know you're a nice man, Mr Miller. Everybody makes mistakes from time to time. I took no offence.'

'Still, I am ashamed of the way I acted. I…'

Miller listened for the voice inside his head to see if it objected to what he was about to say, but it was silent, basking in its recent bloodlust. Miller knew it was as good an opportunity as any to come out and say it. 'What I mean to say is, that I believe you are worth more than this life you currently lead. I would like to take you away from it if of course, you were interested. I-'

She leaned forward and kissed him. For a Moment, Miller was lost in euphoria, it seemed his answer had arrived. No longer would he be without love. And if he had love then he wouldn't need to complete the work he had started. He could be happy, he could have a life and learn to forget the torrid past he had endured. They pulled apart, both smiling awkwardly.

'I've wanted to do that since we first met,' Mary said, folding her hands on her lap.

'Yes, so have i. I've felt an attraction to you that I cannot explain.'

'Sometimes there are no explanations and things are just meant to be.'

Miller could feel the black thing inside his mind starting to stir. He knew what it would want to do if it discovered him alone with a whore, with such a perfect opportunity in front of him. Miller stood. 'For now, I should say goodnight. It is late.'

'Will you see me tomorrow?'

'Of course,' Miller said, knowing that by then word of his exploits would have reached Mary. He hoped she wouldn't connect the blood on him with the work he had done. The excuse of being mugged and attacked in the process was a good one, and he hoped it would hold. Dismissing it, he forced a smile. 'I look forward to us getting to know each other better. Shall I come here tomorrow?'

'No, not here. Meet me in the Ten Bells tomorrow night. Joseph is still paying for this place and if he comes back and finds another man here he'll put me out on the street. The Bells is better.'

Miller nodded. It was likely safer too to meet her in a public place considering what he was capable of doing. He walked to the door, opening it to the chilly air. He turned to face her, her beauty enhanced by the flickering firelight. 'I shall see you tomorrow then.'

He wanted to kiss her again but decided against

it. The thing inside him was stirring and he was as afraid of it as the populace of Whitechapel were afraid of him, an irony which was not entirely lost on him.

'Yes, tomorrow night at the Ten Bells. I look forward to it.' Without another word, he headed down the narrow passage and was swallowed by the darkness. He made his way home, away from the spoils of his labour that night. He knew by now they would likely have discovered the second body and panic would be escalating. For the first time, there was no joy in that idea. The work he had set himself suddenly seemed unimportant, vile, even. Love, he realised was a strange beast. It had, in a short space of time completely changed his outlook and left him with lots to think about.

CHAPTER TWENTY SIX

'You were having second thoughts.' Hapgood said as he prepared a new stack of paper. 'It seems to me you didn't want to kill anymore.'

'At that moment, I would have agreed with you.'

Hapgood frowned, his mouth wavering.

'Say whatever it is that is in your mind, Hapgood. I think I have an idea of the line of questioning to come.'

'There are two questions I wish to ask, if I may. One to further prove your story.'

'Surely you know enough now to be sure I speak the truth?'

'Of course, yet this whole evening has been so surreal I sometimes think it cannot possibly be true.'

'If there is something I can do to further convince you, name it. You will be the one to tell it all. The importance of you believing my words are true is vital. Ask your questions so we can move on.'

Hapgood cleared his throat. 'You mention the wound you inflicted on yourself in error which Mary dressed for you. I imagine such a wound would be deep and leave a scar.'

'Ah, yes, now I understand.' Miller said. 'You wish to see physical evidence. I can oblige your curiosity, Hapgood. Fear not.' Miller stood and removed his outer jacket, which he folded over the arm of the chair. Without it, Hapgood could see how painfully thin he was. Miller walked to the table where Hapgood sat, removing his cufflink and rolling up his sleeve. 'It has faded somewhat with age but still quite visible. Go ahead and look, Hapgood.'

Miller held out a skinny arm. Hapgood leaned closer, heart drumming in his chest as the last shred of doubt as to who Miller was dispersed. Within the tangle of wispy arm hair, the jagged scar on the underside of his left forearm was clearly visible. Thicker at the top and tapering off towards the bottom.

'I was fortunate not to sever an artery. Do you see how it happened?'

Before he could reply and to his absolute horror, Miller moved, giving a macabre physical performance of what had happened. He balled his left fist as if grabbing something. 'I was straddling her of course but for the purpose of this, I shall remain standing. I had a hold of the whore's hair like this at the back of the head. A fistful in my left hand so I could pull it back as I went to work.'

As Hapgood looked on, mesmerised and horrified in equal measure, Miller then made a stabbing motion with his right hand towards the invisible figure he was holding. He went on, lost in the act.

'I stabbed like this. Over and over. Remember, Hapgood, it was dark, and there was a lot of blood. I suspect in my enthusiasm to cause more damage I sliced down my own arm as I targeted the whore's face.'

Miller straightened, breathing heavily at the exertion of activity. It was a perfect example of an old man trying to cling to his youth. 'And so… you see how it happened.' Miller said in breathless gasps. He returned to his seat, struggling to catch his breath. He coughed more blood into his handkerchief and Hapgood struggled to take in what had just happened.

Miller finished coughing and wiped his mouth. 'Does that satisfy your curiosity?'

Hapgood nodded. Words would not yet form.

'Good. You said you had a second question to ask of me?'

Hapgood composed himself, forcing the horror to the back of his mind. 'Yes, I do. I don't quite understand what happened. You talk of love and changing your ways, you talk about a fresh start and a chance at life with a woman who felt the same way as you, and yet less than a month later she would also be dead and in the most brutal of circumstances. I struggle to see how things could have changed so quickly.'

Miller considered for a moment and then stood. He walked to the window, looking out into the night, his back to Hapgood.

He spoke as he stared out into the street. 'I understand your confusion. Even now, so many years later it confuses me equally as much. It is a situation I have thought about every day of my existence and still have no satisfying resolution for other than my original reason for starting my work was correct.'

'The things you did to her, the violence of the attack... How could you go from love to hatred in such a short period of time?'

Miller stared out of the window. Across the street, an alley cat stalked through the sleet in search of food. 'As you will soon hear, something happened which forced my hand as soon as the very next day. I wonder, Hapgood, have you ever felt betrayal? Have you ever experienced an event so unexpected and devastating that it renders you completely shocked?'

'Before this night, no, Mr Miller. That all changed when you came to my door, so I think I can identify with the type of feeling you describe.'

'Ahh, you think so, but when it concerns love and a woman who was supposed to be the one chance to put things right, then before your eyes that is proved to be another lie… then your outlook would be different.'

Miller watched the alley cat disappear into the dark, leaving the street empty, yet he didn't turn around. He continued to stare out of the window, cheeks wet with tears.

'This is your story, Mr Miller, I am simply making a record of it. Feel free to tell me what happened in your own time.'

'Betrayal, Hapgood. Betrayal in the worst possible way. First, it was my mother who betrayed my intentions to protect her. Then later it was Lucy who betrayed me when all I ever wanted was to love her. And then Mary, on the very next morning despite the connection I know we both felt, betrayed me. Tell me, how many times can a man be dealt such a blow and be expected to live with it?'

'I understand the pain, truly I do. What I fail to understand is how the answer you concluded to fix it was brutality. There can be no sane reasoning given for what you did to that woman. There are so many things still unanswered. Why the sudden change? Why was her murder so much more brutal than the rest and if the betrayal you speak of was the very next morning, who the delay before acting on your feelings? Your story is raising many questions, Mr Miller.'

Miller took his blood spattered handkerchief out of his pocket and dabbed his eyes, wiping away the tears. Composed once more, he returned to his seat by the fire.

'You are right, of course. There are many questions to which the answers will soon become apparent. Just know that when I saw her that following morning, when once again my dreams of happiness were crushed beyond all hope, it was clear to me what must happen and what I must do.'

'You seem reluctant to discuss this part of the story.'

Miller adjusted his position, glancing over at Hapgood. 'Even time, I'm afraid, has not eased the betrayal I felt. It burns as strong as ever and know that if not for my body being too broken to continue my work, I would still be on the streets slaying whores for their vile misuse of their bodies.'

Silence befell the room and even with the fire blazing, Hapgood felt a chill brush down his spine at the ferocity in his guest's voice. He was reluctant to ask, but also desperate to hear more of the story. For better or worse, it had utterly transfixed him and drawn him in. 'Please, I would like to know what happened. I feel this could be a vital section of your tale, Mr Miller. If you wish me to write a true account of your life, then it is imperative you leave nothing unsaid.'

'Yes, you are correct,' Miller said, now back to the calm and considered persona he had portrayed for most of the night. 'I shall tell it, and then perhaps even you may understand why I struck next with such ferocity.'

Hapgood made no reply. He knew he would never understand the actions of such a cold and calculated murderer, but was desperate to hear more. He waited in silence, pen ready to write.

Miller composed himself, ready to tell the rest. 'As you recall, I left Miller's court, which, incidentally you will realise is the same as the name I have given you as my own. That, you will learn was no coincidence. That hovel would be my court, and even though Miller is not my true name, justice was served there at my hand.' He glanced at Hapgood who squirmed in his seat at the vile smile spreading across the lips of his guest. 'However, I digress. We will reach that time soon enough. We will pick up the story where we left it. Mary and I had kissed for the first time and I was giving serious thought to stopping my work and trying for a chance at love and true happiness. I returned to my lodgings, giddy with excitement at the future, the deaths of the two whores secondary and almost forgotten initially. I was far too excited to sleep, so after cleaning myself of the blood residue still on my clothes and body, paced the house thinking of scenarios where Mary and I could enjoy our lives together, things we could do, places we could go. I would ask her to leave London with me, to go somewhere new away from the squalor and the city where we both might start again. Even as I thought of happiness, the thing inside me was rousing, perhaps recovering from the initial bloodlust. It wanted us to go back to see our work, to hear the people and how they feared the work we had done. Of course, with Abberline's warning still fresh in my mind I was reluctant, yet I also felt something else. A sense of pride, perhaps. I wanted to see him and know his reaction to what I had done, so I decided we would go and look. We found him where I had left the second whore, the one I had savaged. I saw Godley first, and couldn't see the inspector initially due to the size of the crowd. I took up position across the street, basking in the fear as people talked about what I had done. Even then, my mind was drifting back to Mary and our future together. The work I had done seemed less important than her, and I was, at that point, convinced that I had killed my final whore. There would be no more. That was when I saw him, Abberline, and it was also when my heart exploded, Hapgood. I remember it well, I am certain even now that for a moment, it stopped beating. She was with him. Mary. The two of them speaking by the Yard entrance. I couldn't hear them of course but it was clear what the subject matter was. I remember looking down at my arm that she had so carefully bandaged and knew what had happened. Later, upon finding out about the work I had done, she had understood the true reason I was bleeding and trying desperately to clean myself at that horse trough.'

Miller sneered, gazing at the fire. 'I should have known someone like me would never find happiness. It was clear she had told Abberline about our encounter, and then he, in turn, would come looking for me. If you want to know the reasons for what came next, Hapgood, then know that they were born at that very moment.'

'No.'

Miller looked over to Hapgood, confused as the writer left his desk and crossed the room.

'I don't think that's what happened at all.' he said as he went to his mountain of research and notes on his Abberline book.

'I believe it is my story to tell, Hapgood. How could you possibly know?'

Hapgood found what he was looking for, an old journal. He started to flick through it. 'I don't know anything that is correct. But something I read in Abberline's journals is too close to your recollection to be a coincidence. Here it is.'

Hapgood turned to Miller, who looked on, still confused. 'I appreciate this is your story, Mr Miller, yet I feel obliged at this stage to read this to you. I was convinced I was right before and upon reading again now I am utterly sure. This entry from Abberline's journal tells of that morning too, when he was there at the place where Eddowes was murdered.'

'I have no interest in what the inspector had to

say. Betrayal or not, he did not catch me.'

'Please, Mr Miller, allow me to indulge myself and read this to you. You may find it changes everything.'

'Then read it, Hapgood. Tell me what it is you think is so important I know.'

Hapgood took a deep breath, unsure how what he was about to say would be received. He started to read, afraid of how Miller would react when it was done.

CHAPTER TWENTY SEVEN

Abberline crouched by the body, letting his eyes drift over the carnage. Godley stood some distance away, allowing the inspector the space he needed to assess the situation. Light had started to bleed into the city, and even in the grey overcast light, every grisly detail was visible.

'It's a bloody mess.' Godley said, glancing at the crowds gathering behind the line of officers holding them back. The fear and discontent were clear even from some distance away. 'Two in one night. He's getting bold.'

'This is a message.' Abberline replied as he stood. 'He's done this to prove a point.'

'What kind of point?'

'H meant for this to shock. Look at the marks on the face. He set out to make a mess of this one. He's trying to shock us. Where are those lads to come and take the body away? This lot shouldn't be looking at a mess like this. It's just going to cause more panic.'

'They're picking up the other body then coming to get this one.' Godley took a step closer, looking at the remains on the floor. 'Jesus, it looks like he's cut off her nose.'

Abberline nodded. 'It's going to get worse unless we catch him.'

'How do you know?'

'Each one he kills he's growing in confidence. Each one is more violent than the one before. The first one was more tentative. Uncertain. This one…. This one is the mark of a man confident in what he's doing.'

'What about the one in Dutfield yard? She just had her throat cut. Why leave the other one without mutilation then do this?'

Abberline considered for a moment. He looked at the body then his surroundings. 'I was thinking about that. Initially, I was considering that the two were unrelated and that he only did this one.'

'Maybe he did. We both know whores around here are always in danger from the gangs. If they don't pay protection money they get aggressive.'

'But killing them would be pointless, Godley. How can they pay their money to the gangs if they're dead? No, both of these were done by our man.'

'Then why didn't he savage the other one?'

'I suspect he was almost caught. I think he intended to make just as much of a mess of the other one as this one but before he could he was disturbed.'

'The man who discovered the body said the horse shied away as he entered the yard. Spooked.'

'I suspect our man was still in there at that point, hiding in the shadows and waiting for an opportunity to escape.'

'The body was still warm when it was discovered. She hadn't long been dead. It stands to reason.'

'So our man flees before he can complete his

work how he wanted to. You have to think he was full of rage and desperate to fulfil his needs to the point of risking getting caught, especially with this one.'

'Why especially, Inspector?'

'Look around. That social club was full of people and he did this on their doorstep. He must have been so overcome with rage that the risk was worth taking even when he could hear the people in there singing and having a good time.'

'What do we do now?'

'I want to eliminate that gang idea of yours. Maybe someone in the crowd there knew her and can give us a name.'

'Do you want me to arrange interviews?'

'No, no time for that. I'll handle it.' Abberline said as he walked to the gathering crowds. Expectant and terrified faces stared at him. 'Does anyone know the name of this woman here? Is anyone friends with her?'

Nobody answered. They stared, muttering to themselves. Abberline went on.

'What about gangs? Has there been any word of gang trouble around this area? Somebody must have heard something.'

Abberline watched as the fidgeted. He understood that the lower classes didn't trust the police and as a result, they were reluctant to speak up.

'Please, if anybody knows anything that might help us for God's sake speak up, then I can help make you safe.'

A man stepped forward, his eyes darting. 'I can't say before, but she looks like Catherine. One of the working girls.'

'Do you know her full name?'

The man shook his head. I can't even be sure it's her because of the mess but it looks like her.'

Abberline nodded. 'Thank you. What about gangs? Does anyone have any information on trouble with gangs? Nobody will be arrested, you can speak freely.'

A woman stepped forward, she was delicate with smooth skin and piercing eyes.

'Yes?' Abberline said as she pushed to the front of the crowd.

'I don't know this poor lady or what happened to her, but I know there were gangs working the streets last night.'

'Did you have an an encounter with them?'

The woman shook her head. 'Not me, no. A friend of mine. A man too would you believe? Those gangs are getting bolder.'

'What happened to him, Miss?'

'He was mugged not half a mile from here. He managed to get away but they sliced his arm up with a knife.' She pointed over her shoulder. 'I found him not far from here shaken and cleaning the blood off him in a horse trough. You lot need to police the streets better, it's getting out of hand.'

'I'm not interested in attacks on men. I want to know if any of the girls working the streets had any troubles.'

'Well, you should be worried. Between them and this Ripper, it won't be long before we're all dead.'

A murmur of agreement from the crowd

followed. Abberline looked at them then at her. 'We are doing the best we can. What's your name, miss?'

'Well, it's not good enough. We're living in fear and something needs to be done.'

'And your name?'

'It doesn't matter what my name is. We all feel the same way. What are you going to do to fix it?'

Abberline looked again at the crowd, knowing he couldn't afford to have a baying mob on his hands. He let it go and retreated towards the body where Godley waited. Abberline had always prided himself on his instincts and ability to do his job, yet the more the Ripper murders escalated, the further from a solution he felt.

Hapgood closed the file and stared at Miller. He had remained motionless during Hapgood's reading, staring into the fire which was starting to ebb as it consumed its fuel. The tension was palpable and

Hapgood felt compelled to speak if only to break it. 'As you see, the inspector made extensive notes on his work. When I first read this section it felt like nothing more than an extra detail to use in the creation if his biography. However in light of our conversation tonight, you see that this cannot be a coincidence.'

Miller continued to stare into the flames, his expression neutral. For a split second, Hapgood thought the old man had passed away during the telling, a frightening idea as he would then not hear the rest of the story, which in turn disgusted him and made him feel ghoulish for his selfish interest in hearing it to its conclusion. However, Miller was alive. His chest moved with the regularity of breathing even if his face was devoid of expression. Hapgood felt a pang of fear and tightened his grip on the folder.

'No name.' Miller said, still staring into the flames. 'Abberline mentioned no name of the woman he spoke to.'

'Surely it cannot be a coincidence she relayed

the exact story you told her to hide your actions. On that same day in the same location. That is what you saw, Miller. She wasn't telling Abberline about who she thought you were. She was expressing concern over your fictional attack.'

Miller shook his head. 'No. He would have connected the meeting later when he discovered what had happened at Miller's Court.'

'And how would he have been expected to recognise her after the condition you left her in?'

Hapgood knew he shouldn't have said it, but the words came before he could do anything to stop them. He expected outrage from Miller, but he sat there, trying to come to terms with the idea that everything he knew was false. Hapgood needed to know more. Miller was wrestling with the new information and if Hapgood wanted to relay the story in its truest form, he knew he needed to get the words now when they were most raw and heartfelt. Quietly, he returned to his desk, ready to transcribe. 'Tell me what happened from your point of view.'

Miller sighed. He appeared to have aged even

more in the last few minutes and his eyes for the first time appeared dull and tired. 'I'm not sure I wish to discuss it further. Things have changed and I need time to organise my thoughts.'

Hapgood was desperate to hear more. He was thinking about the fame and plaudits this account would bring him and knew unless it was complete the story was worthless.

'In my experience, it is better to speak of it if you want a true account of the story to be told.'

Miller glared at him, face contorting into a grimace. 'And your potential gain has no bearing on the situation? I wonder who is the true monster here tonight.'

Hapgood flinched, averting his gaze. 'Remember, it was you who came to my door tonight, Miller. You who insisted your tale be heard. I am merely advising you to speak of it and clear your conscience of whatever it is which troubles you.'

'Oh, worry not about discussion. As I sit here an old voice has awoken and we are deep in conversation.'

Hapgood couldn't help but sense the danger. He had, over the course of the night, forgotten who he was sharing the room with. The frail appearance of his guest had disguised the fact that if his account were true, was responsible for the violent and brutal deaths of multiple women. Instinct told Hapgood to run and go for help even if another part of him wondered if Miller was as incapable and weak as he appeared. Perhaps the monster he once was might still be strong enough to kill one more time. In the end, Hapgood's need to know how the story would end took over. He shifted position, banishing the thought of escape and instead pushing Miller to talk.

'There was clearly a misunderstanding between what you thought you saw and what happened. I feel it is important to tell it all, Miller. What happened after you thought Mary had told Abberline about you? Finish the story. Finish and be done with it.'

'Yes, you are right. Let it be told, then, however,

I can only relay it as I know it without taking into account your new information.'

'Yes. I understand. Continue when ready.'

Miller exhaled, once again resuming the guise of a frail old man. 'I saw Mary talking to Abberline and suspected she had told him about me. I have never been comfortable with emotions. Controlling them is something I have always struggled with and this was no different. I had arrived to look upon the scene of my glorious work and walked away filled with confusion and rage....

CHAPTER TWENTY EIGHT

He had felt this before. The ache and bitterness towards humanity. The gnawing agony of betrayal. He had learned to forget those feelings, buried first after discovering his mother's whoring ways then again with Lucy. He realised now as he walked away from the crowd, a passenger as his feet took him without direction through the streets that those feelings had never gone. They were just hidden, buried behind a fragile wall of his own design which now lay in ruins around him. He felt a certain detachment from his surroundings. Neither the cold nor the choking coal and filth stench bothered him. He walked among the desperate, another lost soul in an ocean of misery. The black thing inside squirmed and oozed, thriving on this change in attitude. It was enjoying this new development safe in the knowledge that the shackles which had held it at bay were finally free. Miller knew it had wanted to be in control ever since he was a boy and now he was happy to relinquish all power to it. He passed more of them – whores – standing on street corners in the middle of the day seeking custom.

No more.

He had tried to fight it and live a normal life but knew now it was impossible. His mother had shunned him for trying to help her. Lucy, his one love, the woman he was sure could help him discover a way to defeat his demon had instead fuelled it and fallen into the arms of another. And finally Mary. His one last possibility, his one chance to live in a sense of normalcy had betrayed him in the worst possible way. He arrived at his home, closing out the world, closing out the noise and the stench. Somehow the silence was worse but this, at least, was one problem he knew how to fix. He took the half bottle of scotch from the kitchen table and opened it, drinking without a glass, hoping for the numbing bliss of incapacity to take him before he did something he may regret. It was then, in the silence of his home with rain pattering on the grubby window that the thing inside spoke to him. Miller could sense how much it had grown, how confident it had become.

At last, you see. There was never any other way this could have ended. You must have known.

Miller ignored it. He took another swig of scotch and stared at the wall through blurred vision. He didn't recall when, but at some point, he had started to cry.

Why are you shocked? Did you think she could love you, and you her? A whore and a killer. It would have been doomed.

'You can't be certain.' Miller muttered to the empty room.

Of course, I can. Am I not you? If I think it, then you think it. We are the same. We still have much work to do.

'It is too late. The police will find me. Our work is done.'

You cannot sit here and allow them to take us. There is another way.

Miller took another long drink, knowing what his inner demon referred to.

'No. I will not harm her.'

You still protect her? This whore who has betrayed you?

'She's different,' Miller muttered as he took another drink.

Because she reminds you of Lucy? Another whore who wronged you. This weakness is going to end us.

'It no longer matters. One whore, ten whores, a thousand whores. It will change nothing.'

There is one more whore you must rid from the streets. You know of who I speak.

Miller shook his head and wished the drink would take effect and silence his demon. 'I can't harm her.'

You can and you must. Are not all of our problems related to her? Is she not the poison inside our mind that prevents us from completing more of our glorious work?

'You are the poison. Not Mary.'

He imagined the thing inside his head smirking.

You and I are the same. The difference is you are trapped by the restraints of good conscience. I am the voice of reason. Of desire. Of what you know must be done.

Miller drank again, almost choking on the bitter liquid as it spilt onto his chin. 'I refuse to do it. I will numb you with drink until you are silent once more. Leave me alone to think, damn you.'

Do as you will. You cannot drink me away

forever and I cannot be cut out with that trusty knife of yours. You and I know I always win.

'We shall see.'

Yes. We shall.

Miller drank, trying to ignore the nagging idea that the voice inside him was right about what he would have to do.

You need me. Who else will listen to you complain?

Miller lurched to his feet and staggered towards the bureau, his head already feeling light from the alcohol. He grabbed a journal, tearing out the pages at the front. 'I will write it down,' he grunted at the empty room. 'I shall kill you through drink and write it all down so that I might find the best solution. Do you hear me? You will not win.'

He waited for the thing in his head to respond yet it remained silent. He could sense it mocking him all the same. He was frightened to admit how close he was to the edge. He could see himself tumbling into the abyss and drowning in the blood of whores. Something inside him – perhaps his last shred of humanity- was fighting against it in the hope that he could yet be happy instead of suffering through his existence. He sat at the table and started to write, rambling thoughts and ideas, horrifying visions as they came into his head all the while drinking away the pain. The last rational thought he had that night was that perhaps it would be better if the police did capture him. At least then it would be over. He would be hung and the misery would be at an end. It would, of course, all depend on how much Mary Kelly had told them and in turn how long it would take for them to find him.

CHAPTER TWENTY NINE

The morning light woke him to another overcast day in the squalor of London's East End. A light drizzle fell and its steady tap on the window roused him from a nightmarish slumber of blood and beasts. He was slumped on his table, pen in hand, empty bottle on its side the damning evidence of the previous evening's debauchery. Miller winced as he looked at the words he had written. Now, in the light of day, he was sure someone else had written them. To look over the words and consider such violent ideas had come from his mind was terrifying. However, he did feel better for writing them and decided he would carry on with his journal if it might keep his demon at bay. He glared at the empty bottle on the desk and knew he would need to replace it. Sobriety wasn't a safe state of mind for him when it would bring the dark thoughts of blood and vengeance. It came to him that the double murder he had committed had been almost forgotten, lost in the devastation of what had come after. Despite the risk and knowing Mary Kelly had told Abberline about her encounter with him, Miller had to know how the public had responded to his latest work. One alone was enough to cause panic, and he was curious to see how the feeling on the streets was in response to the two whores he had butchered. He put on his coat and headed out to see what the reaction was to his work.

'It seems your state of mind was compromised during this period.' Hapgood said. He leaned back in his chair and stretched his cramped hand. Miller watched him.

'You look exhausted, Hapgood. I did advise you this would be a lengthy process. To answer your query, yes, there was much uncertainty and confusion. I was sure Abberline would be coming for me and the demon in my mind would not be easily silenced. The days which followed were difficult. I had become a broken shell, ruled by fear and fuelled by the alcohol which kept my inner monster silent. The journal became my only outlet during this time. Despite the violent things I had done, my sole fear was of wondering when

Abberline and the police would come for me. Sleep became a luxury I was no longer afforded and I spent most of my nights drinking myself to a stupor and writing all kinds of depraved things in my journal. That book, if anything, gave the truest insight into whatever lies deep within, deeper even than the account I am giving you here tonight.'

'It would have been interesting to see it.'

'I have it with me in my topcoat. Many of those early rambling pages were removed later when I regained control of my mind yet many pages remain where I talk about my wife and children in ways I do not recall at the time.'

Hapgood glanced at Miller, sure he had misheard. 'Wife? Children? I'm afraid I do not understand.'

'You look surprised, Hapgood. Did you believe my story ended with Mary Kelly?'

'Forgive my surprise. The Mary Kelly murder is known as your final act. I assumed your story would finish there. Certainly, there were no more after.'

'Certainly is a strong term to use. There is much

you do not yet know.'

'More? I believed we were close to the end.'

'Did I not tell you there was much to discuss this evening?'

'Yes you did, but I never expected – '

Miller raised a hand then pulled his handkerchief out of his pocket as another bout of violent coughing came over him. Hapgood waited until he was finished and had tucked the bloody rag into his pocket. 'Forgive me. Speaking for so long is aggravating my condition.'

'We can resume tomorrow if you wish.'

Miller looked at Hapgood, blue eyes burning and inquisitive. 'An hour ago you would have told the police. Now I think you would remain silent if only to hear my tale to the conclusion.'

'I would and I will. You need not tell it all tonight.'

'Ahh, but I must. Although you may well keep your word, my time is short. Life could leave me this very night and what then? With my story unfinished and untold. It has to be tonight,

Hapgood. This has to be the end as there may be no tomorrow for me.'

'I understand. Forgive me, I did not expect you to be married considering all we have so far discussed.'

'You will learn much which will test your opinion of me, Hapgood. Don't be alarmed that even monsters can sometimes find happiness, even if it is short lived. We will get to that point soon enough. I wish to keep my thoughts in order so I may relay it correctly.'

'I understand. Before we continue, if I could ask you about the book. The journal. Would it be possible to see it?'

Miller considered for a moment then stood and walked towards the hallway, his wiry figure appearing to glide in the dancing shadows created by the flickering fire. Hapgood was unable to do anything but stare at the unremarkable book in Miller's hand as he returned. Instead of handing it to Hapgood, he returned to his seat, folding his hands over the closed book.

'May I see it?' Hapgood asked.

'The time is not yet right. There is much of this story still untold and to allow you to read it now would only confuse this tale.'

'I understand.'

'The time will come to read the journal. In fact, it is essential to your completing my story, however, that time is not now. Even so, many of those early pages I spoke of in the immediate aftermath of Mary's perceived betrayal have long ago been removed and destroyed with good reason. Fear not. There remains enough content to give you what you wish to see for your book.'

'What I wish to see?'

'Is it not the wish of the writer to give the reader drama? Controversy? Certainly, during my work, the press were like dogs seeking a new scrap of sensational news to print.'

'I assure you, I deal only in fact. I take my work seriously.'

'As did I,' Miller replied, allowing himself a sly smile. 'I suspect this is why fate has brought us together.'

Hapgood nodded. There was nothing else to say on the subject and even exhausted, he was desperate to hear more of Miller's story. He decided to guide the conversation back towards it, even though the idea of reading the journal and the words of Miller unfiltered by what he chose to say was enticing. 'So you had taken to drinking to keep the demon inside at bay. I imagine that time was difficult for you.'

'It was as you would suspect. For the days that followed the cycle was the same. Days spent drinking and nights without sleep all the while my demon continued to whisper and fight against my desire to be free of it. I remember little of that time, and it seemed the thought of when Abberline would come was lost along with curiosity as to why he yet hadn't. Now, in light of the information you have presented, the reason is clear. However, in my mind and in that of my demon, we had been betrayed. My demon had been waiting for an opportunity to take control and despite my best efforts, it took that opportunity in early November.'

'The night of the Kelly murder.'

Miller nodded. 'My inner demon was furious at my attempts to deny it's needs for so long, and that night without strength left to fight, I gave in and allowed it to take control. You believe you have heard enough of my fury tonight, Hapgood to understand it, but know everything that had come before paled into insignificance next to the rage I felt that night. Without sleep and dishevelled from my almost month-long fight, I was a helpless passenger. I could only watch as my demon took not only the knife we had used for our previous work but several others from my home. We packaged them in paper, and with implements of death tucked under our arm ventured out into the streets of Whitechapel.

'

CHAPTER THIRTY

The night was black, almost as black as the vile thing inside which drove him on in search of blood. He had always considered himself a step above the poor and desperate, yet now as he walked among them as a broken down shell he realised he had never fit in better. Even the stench of them – the poor and desperate – no longer offended him. This was his place, and these were his people. Even though some time had passed since he last struck, it was impossible to ignore the tension in the streets. There was a palpable fear, an expectation that it was a matter of when not if the Whitechapel killer would strike again. The urge to strike at every unfortunate he encountered was strong. The lust for blood had grown from something he could control into a living entity, a force which drove him through the streets as the betrayals he had endured during his life recycled themselves in his mind on a continuous vile loop. He had seen and dismissed several potential targets and knew somewhere in the depths of his mind that on this night, there was only one victim which would suffice. The night was dark, the streets overcrowded with vermin. It was during his third hour of walking that his inner beast, his demon spoke to him, voice thunderous and laced with venom inside his mind.

Why do you continue to delay? You make us walk the streets yet you know where the whore resides. Let us delay no further and be done with it.

Miller was too weak to fight.

You still have doubts, even after she betrayed you. It is only by good fortune we have not yet been captured.

He had no strength to argue. He allowed his demon to guide him towards Miller's Court and what he knew he would find there.

There she is.

Miller stopped on the corner of Thrawl Street, his heart thundering. Mary was a little way down the street talking to a man he didn't recognise.

You see? It was meant to be. You were meant to find her this night.

Miller ignored it, clutching the package of knives tighter and knowing what the contents represented. Unlike with the others, the thought of flaying Mary to the bone didn't fill him with joy or anticipation. It frightened him. If he had been more in control he would have been able to fight, but the beast inside had slumbered for long enough and was well rested. He watched her, grateful that she as in too public a place to act on the vile things the inner him wanted to do. He hated the vile imagery that raced through his mind and as much as he would like to claim no responsibility for them, he knew he and his demon were the same. Its needs and desires were his even if he was reluctant to admit to it.

Remember, she isn't aware you saw her speaking to the inspector. Gain her confidence until you can strike.

'Will she not be afraid of me if she knows what I am?' Miller muttered under his breath.

The whore is likely too drunk to remember. Offer a few pennies to her and see how accommodating she will become.

Miller had no time to say more. Mary had seen him and walked towards him. He expected to see fear, and had he been more in control of his mental faculties, he would have questioned why someone he believed knew who and what he was would approach him and speak without fear if she had informed Abberline of her suspicions.

'Evening, Mr Miller. I didn't expect to see you out so late.'

'I like to walk.' Miller said, allowing the black thing to take control. The sliver of humanity within him still had hope that he could find happiness with her, yet knew it was impossible. His demon was thirsty for blood and he had no power to deny it.

'You picked a night for it. This bloody rain won't stop. I was just heading home.'

'Would you allow me to escort you?'

'I would. Come on then.'

They started to walk.

'Did you hear the ripper struck again? Twice in one night. It's never been safe here but now…everyone is afraid all the time.'

'I did. These are dangerous times.' Miller said.

'What with him and the street gangs it's impossible. How is your arm?'

'Healed now, thank you.'

The inner Miller screamed to be allowed to take control, but in a cruel role reversal the demon pushed him aside, muted him and banished him to the deepest recesses of the brain where he could do no harm.

'I want out of this place. These streets. Some of the girls who work here are good people. They don't deserve this.'

'Nobody forces them to work the streets.'

Mary glanced at him as they walked. 'It isn't something they choose to do. Sometimes it is necessary in order to survive.'

'And would you include yourself in that group who will do anything?'

'Only as a last resort. None of us do this because we like it. When the other option is to die on the streets and hungry, we do what must be done.'

'And if that was no longer the case? If a situation arose where you no longer had to be on the streets and do those things you so hate?'

''Are you propositioning me, Mr Miller?'

Miller smiled. 'In a fashion.'

Mary giggled. She was unsteady on her feet and it was clear she had been drinking. 'Well, I do like you. It isn't often a real man comes around these parts.' She stopped walking, tottering where she stood. She stared at him, and the inner Miller wanted to warn her what was coming. The outer Miller saw his Mother and Lucy as the fire of rage grew hotter in his belly. 'Do you like me?' she asked.

'I would think by now that would be clear. You are special to me, Mary.'

She smiled again, then leaned forward and kissed him. 'Come on then, it's cold.' They walked a little further until she turned into a narrow courtyard, the walls high and close shadows deep and dark - a perfect place to strike had she not been leading him to her lodgings. She stopped outside a corner door.

'Thank you for escorting me.'

'The pleasure is mine.'

She was still drunk and leaned against the closed door. 'Did you mean what you said? That you'd take me away from all this? This live? This desperation.'

'I will if you desire it. I will ensure you never again have to do those things which you hate.'

She blinked then looked away as she fought to hold back tears. 'Look at me, crying. I don't even have a handkerchief.'

Miller took his own red handkerchief out of his pocket - the same one he had tied around his own neck to hide the scratches from his last victim - and handed it to her. She took it and dabbed her eyes. 'Thank you. I don't know what came over me.'

'You have no need to apologise to me.'

She took his hand in hers. Miller noticed how cold it was. 'Would you like to come in? I warn you, it isn't much. Just a fireplace and a bed, but it's dry and will soon warm if we get a fire lit.'

'I would like that very much.'

Mary unlocked the door and led him in. Miller closed it after them, isolating them from the world.

CHAPTER THIRTY ONE

The room was exactly as Mary had described. A grubby single space dominated by the bed pushed up against the wall in the corner. A bedside table housed a few belongings and there was an open fireplace, only a few glowing embers remaining. Mary tottered to the fireplace. 'It will soon warm up in here as soon as I get this fire going.'

'Please, allow me to do that.' Miller said as he set his wrapped package on the bedside table.

'Ever the gentleman,' Mary replied, allowing him to take over. She sat on the bed as Miller built the fire. 'You live here alone?' he asked as he worked at building the dying embers into something more substantial.

'I do. I used to share it with a man, but that is finished now.'

'You're sure he will not return and inquire why I'm here with you at this hour?'

'Not a chance. Joseph is a good man at heart but he didn't like it when I sometimes let the girls stay here. Just to get them off the streets when they didn't have money for a doss. He used to tell me he didn't want it to become some kind of whorehouse.'

The flames were starting to build, giving a dull orange glow to the room. Miller took the iron poker from next to the fireplace and stoked the coals, encouraging them to take.

'That was why he left. He said that if I intended to make this place a whorehouse it would be without him and h wouldn't support it, so he left.'

'I see,' Miller said as he added more fuel to the fire, warming his cold hands on the growing flames.

'Of course, he wasn't an understanding man like you.'

'Edward. Please. I believe we no longer need to be so formal.'

'Of course, Edward, then. See he didn't understand how it was out there. Not like you. You know how hard it is.'

Miller didn't answer. He continued to stoke the fire. Mary sighed and lay on the bed. 'That's coming up nicely. It will soon be warm in here I expect.'

Miller again chose not to reply. In his mind's eye, he was seeing blood and imagining the vile things he was about to do knowing there was no disturbing them. No time constraints to prevent his work from taking the shape it deserved. Mary started to sing where she lay on the bed. It was the classic song of the drunk, a warble which although tuneful was hardly masterful. Miller stoked the fire, wondering if it would be possible to push the hot poker up her so far it would come out into her throat and burn her vocal chords. He smiled at the thought, a private expression only for the flames to see. He set the poker aside, satisfied with the work he had done. The room now had a healthy orange glow as the temperature rose. Miller stood, brushing his hands on his legs as he did. 'I think that will do the trick.' He said, staring at Mary who may on her back. Eyes closed as she continued to sing.

She opened one eye and giggled. 'Come on then, I won't bite.'

'You are certain we won't be disturbed?'

'Of course, I am. You can lock the door if it will make you more comfortable. The key is on the table there.'

Miller stood and took the key, unable to believe how easy it was. He locked the door as Mary started to sing again. He stood by the door, watching her croon with her eyes closed. Waiting for him. His eyes flicked to the package containing his knives.

'These are dangerous times on the streets with the Ripper murders being so frequent.'

Mary ignored him, still singing. He walked towards her pausing to pick up his package before sitting at the foot of the bed. 'I would like to tell you a story. Something I have never said to anyone else.'

She continued to sing, now moving on to a haunting melody which was beautiful even if she was worse for drink.

'You see, for many years I have been a lonely man. One troubled by a childhood which was unstable and filled with horror. You remind me of people from my life, individuals who have influenced the man I would become.'

He glanced over to see if she was paying attention, but the heat had made the influence of the alcohol more complete, and she was slurring her words as she sang.

'First, there was my mother. A woman I respected. A woman I always thought would keep me safe. I discovered at a very early age that this woman who I believed I knew was an impostor. A vile creature who did despicable things. My father knew. He encouraged it. Now as an adult I'm certain he forced her to do it, at least in the beginning. As abusive and vile as he was, she protected him. She shunned my attempts to save her from the horrors she endured. She was vulnerable, or at least she was to me as a child. I see the same vulnerability in you. An innocence buried deep because that is the only way you can exist.'

'Are you going to get into this bed or sit there talking all night,' she slurred. Miller closed his eyes and stilled the rage. He started to unwrap the package he had brought with him.

'When my father abandoned us, I always thought things would be better. Yet my mother blamed me for him leaving. She said if I had kept quiet, he wouldn't have gone. Can you imagine, a violent drunk who dominated everyone in his life thought of as someone to be missed? Even so, missed he was, by her at least, and my mother and I became estranged. It would be some years later when all hope was lost that I met someone who I was sure would take the pain away that lived inside me.'

Mary was still singing. Miller set the package next to him and opened it out on the mattress by her feet. He took great care in lining up the vast array of knives, ensuring the handles of each were level. He glanced over his shoulder to see if she had noticed them yet, but she was oblivious, eyes closed in her own world. The heat was becoming quite intense from the fire. Miller took off his topcoat and folded it over the bottom of the bed. 'Her name was Lucy. You have many similar features. The same delicate nose, the same eyes filled with curiosity. Sadly, like my mother, my experience with Lucy would be a bitter one. I opened myself to her, gave her all the love I had, an emotion new to me then. I gave her it all and she fell into the arms of my best friend.'

Miller selected a knife, the one had used to kill the others so far, the six inch blade shimmering in the light of the fire. 'It was then when I knew I was never destined to be happy, never destined to be like everybody else. My calling was different. For a time, I thought it was a calling from God. A great work to be done at his request. I have since come to believe this is not the case. This cannot be the work of God as such a being who claims to love all humankind equally cannot exist in a world so filled with misery and pain. This is a world for demons, a world for those willing to do whatever it takes to further their own interests no matter the consequences.'

He turned towards her on the bed, showing her the knife and waiting until she opened her eyes. She stopped singing, almost falling asleep until he touched the steel to her leg. She opened her eyes and looked at him her smile fading as she saw the knife in his hand. He set the blade down with the others and turned back to face her. 'And now, at last, you know what I am. I cannot give you the love you desire, but one promise I will keep is that you will never again flaunt your wares on the streets, Lucy. Never again will you run to George and find comfort with him.'

'I don't understand, who is Lucy? What are you doing?' Miller stared at her, waiting for her drink addled mind to catch up and process what was happening. He saw it happen, the flicker of understanding. 'Oh, Murder….' She said. It was all she could manage before he lunged at her She was powerless to stop him. He was too quick and she was too drunk. He clamped his hands around her throat, squeezing as she clawed at him. Miller looked at her face and saw his mother, he saw Lucy. He saw betrayal and a symbol that love for him could never happen. All women in his life had failed him and now they would pay. He straddled her, watching the vessels in her eyes bloom and turn the whites of the eyes red as he crushed her windpipe. She was so delicate she was under his grasp, a fragile thing, the hatred he had held onto since he was a child at last released. He blinked, realizing only then he was crying as he took life from her, watching as the spark faded and her eyes became glassy and sightless. Even when she stopped struggling he didn't let go. Cheeks wet with tears he leaned close and kissed her on the forehead then whispered in her ear. 'If any of your soul remains, just know I have saved you from what is to come. He released his grip, staring at her body as it lay on the bed. He could only see Lucy when he looked at her and every passing second increased the ferocity of his anger. He walked to the window and looked out into the black night. It was only a few hours until dawn but Miller was in no hurry. The fire inside was as hot and stifling as the one in the room and he knew it was time to go to work. He pulled the curtains closed, ensuring nobody could see into the room. The steel kettle by the fire he filled with water so he could wash after it was done, then he undressed, folding his clothes and placing them on the floor by the door. He then stoked the fire, filling the grate with as much coal as possible to ensure the theatre for his work was illuminated to the fullest.

'Do you remember me, Lucy? Do you remember when you said I wasn't a man? He picked up his knife and approached his canvas, finally ready to let it out. The rage, the fury at the wrongdoing he judged to have happened to him during his life. He went to work, the frenzy within him total as he took a lifetime of frustration on the corpse of Mary Kelly. His recollections came in snatches of clarity through the mist of fury so pure, so intense that it was unlike anything he could have ever imagined.

Flaying her thigh to the bone, the white shaft surrounded by red meat.

Exposing her delicate breasts, then remembering how Lucy had shown hers to him and chastised him for not being a man, hacking them from the body, one first then the other, setting them on the bedside table with other fleshy parts he had removed.

The kettle whistling over the raging fire, a sound secondary and ignored to the cyclone of fury in his head.

Hacking at her abdomen, cutting it away, slashing at the essence of what made her a woman, the thing she used to entice men into her web. He obliterated it, hacking and slashing, gouging it until her entire lower half was an unrecognizable pulp.

Staring into her eyes, and seeing Lucy, still mocking, still belittling him to the point he couldn't stand it anymore. Slicing off her nose, then hacking at her face, a crisscross of slashes, the blade embedding in bone, the dull pop as his knife cut through an eyeball, leaving a trail of fluid to mingle with the bloody remains of her face, the features no longer recognizable, and her no longer staring or mocking him.

Pulling everything out hacking with his knife and cutting the heart free. Placing it in the fire along with her clothes to further stoke the flames, the kettle now a melted twisted thing drooping by the grate.

Something breaking. A distinct snap in his mind, a severing of the rage.

Him falling to his knees by the bed, drenched with blood and sweat, exhausted. So much blood. It was everywhere. The walls, the floors, the woman barely recognizable.

He took her hand and lay it across what remained of her stomach cavity, then there was silence apart from the fire and the steady drip of the blood which had soaked through the mattress and was falling from the bed frame to the floor, where it gathered in small pools. He listened for the inner voice, to see what it made of the work that had been done, but it was gone, the two melded into one by the ferocity of the act he had just committed.

He stood and walked to the fire which had reduced now to a mound of smouldering coals. Using the poker, he removed the shrivelled remains of the heart then scooped it up in his handkerchief, tying a knot into it to keep his prize safe. The room was silent and in the almost near dark he could see the ambient light through the cracks in the curtains had brightened by a few shades. He had lost all sense of time and realised he had been at work for so long daylight was now close. He grabbed a man's shirt from the dresser - no doubt one belonging to Mary's former lover - and used it to clean as much of the blood from his hands and face as possible before tossing the bloody garment into the guttering fire. The heat devoured the material, briefly illuminating the room and the work he had done as it ravaged the shirt. He then dressed, unable to shake the feeling inside.

There was no elation. No sense of a job well done. He turned his senses inward and could feel nothing. No rage. No overwhelming urge to destroy those who had wronged him. He even searched for the part of him he had locked away but he too was gone leaving whatever remained as a broken shell of a man. A soulless thing. He finished dressing, collected his knives and rewrapped them in the paper package, then took the key from the dresser beside the pile of parts he had cut off, then quietly unlocked the door and went outside, locking the door behind him. The alleyway was deserted, and pulling his cap down over his eyes, he disappeared into the night, slipping the key into his pocket with the handkerchief containing the blackened stub of shrivelled heart. Once again he was alone in the world.

Hapgood exhaled and set the pen down, he rubbed his eyes with the palms of his hands. He had gone beyond fatigue, and the combination of tiredness and the mental exhaustion of listening to Miller's tale had combined to devastating effect. Miller said nothing. He watched Hapgood and appeared curious to see what the biographer would say next.

Hapgood cleared his throat then stood, his legs shaky from overtiredness. 'I think another drink is in order.'

Miller again remained silent as Hapgood refilled his glass. He held the bottle towards Miller, but the older man shook his head. Hapgood stood by the fire, unable to look at it without recalling the tale he had just been told. He suspected it would stay with him forever. He took a sip of his drink.

'You seem quite shaken.' Miller said.

'That was some story. It is a lot for the mind to process.'

'I understand. I did advise you on arrival, Hapgood that there was a lengthy tale to be told.'

'It is not the length but the content which disturbs me so.' Hapgood drained his glass then set it on the mantle. He turned to Miller, eyes red and stinging from overtiredness. 'May I ask you a question?'

Miller nodded.

'What you said about feeling nothing. About feeling broken inside. Is that why you stopped? After Mary Kelly, you disappeared never to be seen again.'

Miller considered the question, drumming his fingers on the journal on his lap. 'Something did change in me that night. There is little doubt about that. At the time I had little knowledge as to why. The intervening years have given a little insight. I suspect the ferocity of my actions, the outpouring of frustration and betrayal presented itself there in that room. Indeed, when it was done I felt like there were no longer opposing sides of my personality. There was no more light attempting to wrestle with the dark for control. When it was done there was just one entity remaining. The desire to destroy had been sated completely. The fire extinguished at last inside me.' Miller half smiled - a wicked curl of the lip which frightened Hapgood. 'Or at least, that was the case for a while.'

'It came back? The fire?'

Miller raised a skinny hand. 'We will come to that. First, allow me to finish the thought. When I left that night and walked through those darkened streets in a daze, knowing inside I was a changed man. Clarity of thought, if you will. Remember, Hapgood, this incident happened without the information you presented to me earlier in regards to the nature of Mary's conversation with Abberline. With the fire inside quelled, the reality of the situation as I saw it presented itself and brought fresh concerns.'

Hapgood nodded in agreement. 'Of course. As you understood it, she had told Abberline who she suspected you were and you had….done those things to her. It was natural to expect you would be soon arrested.'

Miller nodded. 'I became convinced Abberline would be coming for me. How that man plagued my nightmares for many months after, Hapgood. Can you comprehend how it felt to a young man as I was filled with certainty that somebody was looking for you? Let me assure you it wasn't pleasant. I knew I had to leave the area. I knew once they found what I had done, they would come for me'

'So you left Whitechapel before they could get to you. That's why the killings stopped so suddenly.'

Miller nodded, fixing his gaze on the biographer for a moment, then staring into the ebbing fire. 'I had lived within the means at my disposal and had saved much of the money Lucy had sent me. There was enough for me to ensure I would not be found.'

'Where did you go?'

'I took a steamer to America. I had no idea what to expect when I arrived there, but it was far away from my old life. As the vessel pulled away from the dock and left the soot-covered warrens of Whitechapel behind, I watched from the deck as the only life I had ever known as it slipped into the past, and with that, the story you know is finished, Hapgood, yet there is still more to tell. The part no man alive has ever been told before. I promised you a story which would be the biggest of your career, Hapgood and you shall have it. You will be the first man to learn what came after Whitechapel.'

'Your life in America.' Hapgood muttered, unable to comprehend what was happening.

'Indeed. You will learn that although I left my old life behind on that vessel, demons are impossible to outrun no matter how far you go. For a while, that inner beast was satisfied with the blood it had feasted on. But like any animal, its instincts would soon present themselves again. I doubt most will believe it, but I did try to live a regular life there and would have if not for my demon, a burden I have lived with since birth. He's a devious beast, Hapgood. Sometimes he presents himself without my knowledge and takes control. Perhaps it is fortunate that my physical body is broken. Only because of this has the beast been caged forever, trapped in a vessel that cannot do the things it once did. Are you ready to continue?'

'I believe so. This has come as a shock as I'm sure you can appreciate. Allow me to prepare new paper.'

'Of course.' Miller said. He stood and stretched then crossed to the window, looking out into the darkened street. He then walked to the fireplace and picked up the poker and stoked the coals. Hapgood watched him and felt a pang of terror as he placed this visual with the account Miller had given of the Mary Kelly murder. Miller stoked the fire, then looked at the photographs on the mantle above it. He picked one up and turned to Hapgood. 'Your wife?'

Hapgood stared open-mouthed. Miller saw the fear and smiled, setting the photograph back. 'Have no fear, Hapgood. Surely you realise now I mean her no harm? Can you not see I am incapable of acting on the beast's instructions? I was merely asking a question.'

'Yes. That is my wife.'

'I will tell presently of my wife. I recall you were curious to know more when I made mention of it earlier tonight. First, to answer another curiosity you had. Miller took his journal approached Hapgood. The writer stared at it, nervous and afraid for what it may contain. 'This illustrates better than any words I can say my immediate state of mind following my leaving Whitechapel. I wrote these opening pages on the If you truly wish to know the Ripper, then this is where you will find him. Beware, Hapgood, this is not the same man you have met here tonight. If you want to know the monster rather than the man, then this is where you will find him. He lives within these pages laid bare and at his most vile. If you choose to read it, you will meet the bastard thing we have discussed in such depth this evening in person.'

Miller handed the journal over. Hapgood stared at it but did not open it. 'Am I to read it now?'

'The post Whitechapel years were difficult. I would rather not talk about them unless necessary. Here, at least, you will see the rest of the tale. Go ahead, Hapgood. Read and understand how the beast that plagues me behaves and thinks. See how it is to have to endure the burden of such a monster and perhaps you will begin to understand.'

Hapgood touched the journal, his hands shaking. He realised that until that point, he had known this story and had some idea of the direction it would take. What he was about to read was a step into the unknown, and would give the first true glimpse of who Miller truly was. Hapgood composed himself and opened the journal.

CHAPTER THIRTY TWO

At last, I am finished.

As this ship which I boarded two days ago makes its way across the Atlantic, I feel the glow of satisfaction that my work is complete. How the blood, so sticky and warm, covered every inch of the filthy hovel of hers. If they feared me before they cannot comprehend the horror of what I have left for them to find.

If only the other passengers knew who was in their midst. I nod and smile and make polite conversation. Little do they know they converse with the Whitechapel fiend and that in my bag is the Kelly woman's heart, wrapped in my handkerchief and tied with string.

It amuses me to speak with these people. Just this afternoon I engaged in a lengthy discussion about the Jack the Ripper murders with a chap named Roberts. He was full of hope that the police would catch the murderer, and that he was glad to be away from the capital and the horrors which dwelled within. I suggested to him that perhaps The Ripper had concluded the same as he, and was on this vessel with us and fleeing London. His vexed expression amused me so.

Ahh, my work.

My one regret is that Lucy does not know it was I who was responsible for the Whitechapel murders and all the blood I have spilt is because of her.

Death to whores, those who peddle their filthy wares, spreading disease!!

There is a new calmness within me. For now, the fire appears quenched as the demon slumbers. So to a new life in America I go. During this monotonous journey, I find my thoughts drifting to my father, at how he turned to drink much in the same way I had started to during the height of my work. That is something I must control, and with my new life in America, I will. My father could not. He was weakened, perhaps by the things he made my mother do. Drink, it seems, was the only way he could blot out the pain of the whore's actions. Even I, a small child was not exempt from his vile actions. Sometimes, he would come into my room when he was drunk. I would lay still and pretend that I was sleeping, praying he would leave me alone. Sometimes he would just sit there and watch me. Other times... he would do things I will not commit to paper

Three days ago I threw my knife in the Thames and with it my old life. It is time to start again.

December 18th, 1889

Has it been a year? How time has passed. Much has happened since I arrived across the water. This journal had been untouched, forgotten until we moved to this new home and now rediscovered in my office.

I have taken a wife.

That which had left me, that which I thought I would never be able to have, found me soon after I arrived in this new world. She has three children already, and her former husband died leaving her a widow. She does not remind me of Lucy or my mother, and her presence has helped to keep the demons I harbour inside hidden and silent.

Love is everything I ever imagined. Being away from the filth of Whitechapel and the memories it kept has changed me as a man as much as it is possible to change. I still fight those demons of course. That is a battle which will go on until I take my final breath, but with Josephine and the children by my side, I can control it. I have taken the children on as my own and they call me father. The girl, her daughter, is also called Lucy! The irony does not escape me. This new life so full of uncertainty when I set out to it has been like a gift to me. Josephine is wealthy, her husband a rich man before his passing. She is so in love with me that she has given me full control over the family assets and we have purchased this most luxurious of homes, a property a far cry from the filthy hovels of Whitechapel.

Christmas draws closer. It is strange to celebrate it amid such humid conditions which I have still not grown accustomed. The heat is oppressive; however, the new house is spectacular, offering a view of the Florida coastline which mere words cannot adequately describe.

The ocean is a wonderful blue-green and shimmers like gemstones under the heat of the sun, which itself soothes me and is working wonders on my aching, tired bones. You may think I am unable to appreciate things such as beauty; however, these are not at all alien to me. The children are excited. To them, this new home represents an adventure – if only it were the same for me, as despite my new found happiness, I still feel a sullen emptiness left by the absence of my work. I try not to think of such things, yet a whispered voice deep inside occasionally reminds me of those old desires. I dismiss those whispers with some effort and endeavour to continue to keep focus on the joys of this new life I have been gifted.

I may take up painting and express myself through art. Josephine says it is a superb idea, however, I am fearful of what macabre images may translate from brain to paintbrush. Perhaps some other creative project would be more suitable?

December 26th

A darkness has overcome me.

These spells have recently increased in both frequency and intensity. I know their origin, of course. It is that thing. The beast inside me is starting to stretch ready to wake from it's enforced slumber, which I find both terrifying and intriguing. I find with each passing day my attention on the present wanes and I reflect more on my life of old. The children are playing with their toys, and the urge to unleash my rage at the noise is proving difficult to withstand.

Violence is at the forefront of my mind at all times. I took my wife violently last night, clutching her throat. It reminded me of my work with the whores and excited me in ways I had begun to forget. She has, so far, avoided contact with me this morning, raising no questions as to the finger marks on her neck. I rule this house, and each of them knows their place.

I may need to go for a walk to clear my head. It is cooler today and overcast, more like the English climate I am accustomed to. As I watch the children playing, bizarre visions of cutting off their hands and removing their tongues flicker in my mind. My heart races, yet I am still. Even managing a smile as Oliver shows me his toys.

I have decided after all to take up painting. I hope that it will provide an outlet for my frustration.

January 1st

I miss Abberline. It pains me to say it, but I find myself wondering if he is still looking for me. I feel better than in recent weeks. I have taken to long walks in the evenings, wondering the streets as I dwell on my thoughts. They are a far cry from the streets of Whitechapel. I tried to imagine doing my work here; continuing where I left off, but I cannot compare the two. This God forsaken heat even in what should be winter is unbearable. I crave the chill of a winter night, the inky darkness of the streets of London...and yes. The whores.

Without my work to consume me, I feel at a loss. I try to devote myself to my children and wife but cannot find solace even in their comfort. I scoured the papers today, looking for news on myself, and was saddened that I was nowhere to be found. That voice deep within is speaking again, but I have the will to silence it for now at least.

CHAPTER THIRTY THREE

'You were starting to lose control again.' Hapgood said as he looked up from the journal.

Miller had barely moved. Hapgood pressed him. 'That first Christmas with your new wife and children. Those old desires had awoken.'

'That fire was one I knew would never be extinguished, Hapgood, as much as I would have liked nothing more.'

'The way you have written…it appears you were curious as to what would happen.'

Miller shrugged. 'Perhaps I was. Remember, Hapgood, a great void had been left by the absence of my work. I stumbled upon love with Josephine, and like with Lucy before her, I always hoped the love of a woman would fill the void enough so that the desire to do those things no longer existed.'

'Instead, it only quelled them temporarily.'

Miller nodded. 'Indeed it did. Please, ask me no more of it, Hapgood. Not yet. Leave me to contemplate my thoughts. Read on. You still have much to learn.'

Hapgood opened his mouth to say more, then thought better of it. He wanted to know what happened next in Miller's incredible tale, and so returned his attention to the book, turning the page and reading the next entry.

January 4th

I dreamed of death last night. A mountain of skulls upon which I sat naked, as a rain of blood poured from a crimson sky. I woke aroused and took my wife as she slept despite her protests upon waking at my forced intrusion. I had to silence her by covering her mouth, and for a moment, I saw Eddowes, then Kelly Before I cut off her nose. She tried to squirm free and I told her that unless she wished me to slit her throat to the bone, she would be silent and allow me to finish what I started.

Afterwards, she looked at me like I was a monster, but I do not care. I find myself becoming more and more withdrawn, and have begun to get headaches, blinding pain behind the eyes which leaves me incapacitated. I blame her, the whore of a wife who will not bow to my will. Perhaps I should show her the truth and allow her a glimpse into the darkest reaches of my mind?

I'm tempted but know I cannot. Tomorrow I shall buy paints and canvas and attempt to recreate the imagery from my dream. I must snap myself out of this ever dark mood. If I raise suspicion, it is not out of the question that I could be connected to my old work back in Whitechapel.

Our neighbour, Gloria is fond of learning of things which do not concern her and seems to exist to know the business of others. If she gets too close I shall tear out her eyes and feed them to her.

One of my headaches is coming. As I write I can feel it growing behind my eyes. I will stop now, and try to sleep in the hope that it will pass. I tire of writing in this book. It makes little sense.

April 11th, 1890

Just over a year has passed since my last entry into this journal. It appears I had made my last entry from a dark place, which I am pleased to say has brightened somewhat. Art has been my saviour. The fruits of my old work have been replaced with the joy of the new. I have converted the downstairs study into a studio of sorts, one which is off limits to my wife or children. Even the housekeeper knows that despite the chaotic state it is to remain undisturbed. Despite the fear I would embrace the macabre, much of my work is quite the opposite. Glorious and lush landscapes, sunset from the beach, flowers in a vase by the window. It seems I have quite the eye for detail. The one piece of dark work which I did commit to canvas now hangs alone on my studio wall. My wife despises it, but her feelings mean nothing to me. It is MY work, and MY study, and I shall hang on the walls whatever I please.

It is the scene from my dream. A lone figure stands atop a mountain of skulls, a curved blade in his left hand. His face is in shadow, one white eye visible. In his right hand, he holds five severed heads which although vague in detail, are the Whitechapel whores as red rain falls from a crimson sky.

It is by far my favourite piece, the only true expression of what lives within me.

November 3rd

I have gained weight. I don't look after myself as I should, however, November is a month which is dear to me. It reminds me of my work, of happier times. It seems that my patience is wearing as thin as my hairline. How could it be that without the burden of being hunted by the police, I feel more strained? Not for the first time, I wonder about Abberline. I like to think he too keeps journal such as this one, and wonders about me. He was the closest thing I had to a nemesis, and one cannot fault his determination to apprehend me. It feels as if our business has been left unfinished, and if I desire one thing it is to look at him and remind him of what he said to me that day at the police station about how incapable of being a monster I was. Oh, for him to know the truth would fill me with joy! Perhaps I will head back to London and re-ignite his fire? Just a quick kill to remind them I am still here and then back over to America. If only it were an option. However, I fear that such a move would only serve to fully awaken that which has remained dormant and I fear the day that happens. I must stay strong.

December 20th

I can no longer live like this. I have not picked up a paintbrush in weeks, the joy seems to have left me as quickly as it had arrived. Something dark is stirring within, and it is with excitement and reservation I wait to see what happens. Oliver came over to me today to speculate as to what gifts he would receive for Christmas. I suggested perhaps he would receive a knife, not unlike Jack the Ripper's with which he could hound his friends and cut out their tongues when he caught them.

My wife didn't see the joke, however, and regarded me with a look with which she will regret later this evening. Perhaps I will take a knife to her and cut her. Oh, to see fresh blood oozing from broken skin would be a delight.

She thinks I don't know what she is doing. But I know all. I see her, deep in whispered conversation with that bitch from next door. Could she suspect me? Perhaps they both know. It isn't too much of a stretch of the imagination and they are keeping their silence until Abberline arrives across the ocean to apprehend me and cast those knowing eyes on me, smug that at last I have been captured. I will not stand for this, not after all I've done to leave that life behind. I must find out.

December 21st

The whore knows nothing, I am now certain of that. If she did she would have told me during the beating I gave her. I felt little guilt for the things I did to her. She should not imply with her actions to be conspiring against me. I was forced to take the action I did as I feared that otherwise the truth would be hidden. I'm afraid to say her face is quite the picture, and I'm sure that come morning, she will have some wonderful bruises for her and the cunt next door to discuss. God help her if she crosses me again.

Straddling her and seeing the blood come from her mouth and nose caused the slumbering thing inside me to stir. It has started to whisper to me about dismembering the children and I have been inclined to listen to its argument. I have also started to drink again. With its help I hope I can blot out the numb emptiness within, however, alcohol fuels the rage and shortens my temper even further. I feel ready to explode. I try to recall my work, the days when life seemed oh so simple and realise I miss it. I need to do something.

I'm suddenly tired, but know all too well that I will not find sleep next to the whore and her pained moans. I will sleep here in my study. It seems to be the only place in which I feel able to be myself.

December 29th

Another New Year dawns, and yet, I ache to relive the past. I could deny it, but there is little point. I crave the attention. I desire the thrill of the chase. Most of all I miss the blood.

I sometimes wonder if this is my punishment, my personal hell in which I am forced to live a normal life without indulging in my work. I sometimes wonder how many of the filthy whores now infest Whitechapel. Many more than there would be if I were still there to take care of my work that much is for certain. However, as always, I will not to dwell for too long on such matters, and try to move forward.

Somebody is at the door; I can hear their muted voices from out in the hallway. I will not be going to greet them, my study has become my refuge, and only within its walls do I feel safe. I think somebody has been in this room. I'm sure that the papers on my desk have moved since I was last here. Perhaps it was one of the children – and if so I will need to hand out a dose of punishment. This is MY place and is off limits to all. However, they are children and know only what they have been taught. If I find that the bitch Josephine has been rummaging amongst my possessions, she will feel the full force of my fury.

I grow weary of her as each day passes, and sometimes wonder where the love I once had for her has gone. I see the way she looks at me as if I were some kind of animal, and I suspect that she is attempting to turn the children against me. With God as my witness, she will not do to my children as my whore mother did to me. I will kill her before that happens, rip her insides and show them to her as I watch the life ebb from her eyes. Perhaps as she faded into the arms of death, I would whisper my dark secret to her, give her something to think about as she tumbles into hell.

I am angry, and I can hear the excited chatter of our visitor, the stupid bitch from next door.

She is also fortunate that I don't rip her like I did Nichols. I wonder if she would even cease to chatter as her innards spilt onto the ground. If I am lucky perhaps one day I will find out. Until then I must remain focused on maintaining my calm.

I have sent some of my paintings to be shown in an exhibition in France. I had toyed with leaving my favourite piece on the wall of my study, but at the last moment had decided to send it along with the others. Perhaps the French will appreciate my dark inner imagery.

CHAPTER THIRTY FOUR

Hapgood looked up from the journal, skin pale, eyes ringed dark through fatigue. To his surprise, Miller was staring at him, his own expression neutral. 'You see me now for the first time for who I am, don't you, Hapgood?'

'The things you have written are disturbing, to say the least. I am reluctant to read more. It feels inappropriate to read on as some kind of ghoulish voyeur.'

'And yet you will. It is far too late to deny the level of curiosity you have for my story, Hapgood. I can see in those tired eyes of those the curiosity to see more. Besides, everything you are reading now is long in the past. There is nothing you or I can do to change those events.'

Hapgood forced a weak smile. 'You are correct. I feel I should indulge no further, yet your story has captivated me. I fear I have become a slave to it until I reach its conclusion.'

'Then allow me to delay you no further. Read on, Hapgood. Indulge the curiosity and know the rest of my tale. The first light of day will be with us soon. It has been a very long evening for us both.'

Hapgood glanced at the drinks cabinet and considered pouring another and then decided a sober mind was the best way to approach his task. He turned the page and was once again lost in Miller's world.

January 11th, 1891

I am in France.

The climate here is much more tolerable compared to the sticky humidity of the Americas, and it has lifted my spirits. Josephine and the children are still in America. They wanted to come but I forbade them. I'm sure the bitch wonders what I will do when left to my own devices.

The reason for my visit here is to meet a gentleman by the name of Rene. He is interested in purchasing some of my paintings and insisted on meeting me face to face. I could not wait to accept his invitation to visit the French countryside, as I was sure that the house in America was somehow driving me to insanity. Already I feel refreshed and able to think without the chatter of the whore and the whine of the children.

January 13th

I write this from a beautiful golden beach looking out over the ocean. The weather is too cold for tourists, and so I sit alone, with only this trusty journal for company. My meeting with Rene went well, and I was surprised to find that he appreciated my work. His main interest was my favourite piece, the scene from my dream. I was reluctant to sell, yet after some persistence, a fair price was negotiated and I have agreed to give him a few extra days to look over my other works to see if there were any other pieces of interest. It was an empty gesture of course. He and I both knew there was only one painting that was worth his attention, but the extra days mean I do not yet have to venture back to that tomb of a house and the strangers who reside there.

I look out over the channel, beyond the rolling tide and fantasize that I can see England. My heart races at the thought of going back to Whitechapel. It is so close yet so far away. Would those streets remember me the way I remember them? I believe so.

January 15th

I have arrived in London. I knew I would regret it if I did not make even a short journey to visit the site of my work. I feel more alive than at any time since I left this labyrinth of cobbled streets and poverty. A light drizzle falls outside the window to this lodging, yet it cannot dampen my spirits. Could this be how true love feels? Could filthy, whore infested streets stir in me the emotions that my family cannot?

I am only a short distance from where I did the Nichols bitch. Perhaps I will take an evening stroll past where I left her fat, bleeding corpse.

January 27*th*

I am back in America, yet my heart is filled with the joys of my secret visit to Whitechapel, and I mourn it like the death of a loved one. I spent two glorious days walking the twisting labyrinths and deep shadows which gave the comfort I craved. The beast stirred as expected and I allowed it to whisper its vile ideas and found myself not in outright disagreement at the suggestion. I was propositioned by whores at every turn, and why not? After all, I am a respectable gentleman. The filthy wretches have long forgotten about me and my work. When I left, fear hung in the air like a thick and potent presence. Now it is gone and I'm both sad and furious. The temptation to kill was high, but I did not act upon my desires.

I did follow one filthy bitch as she walked the maze of stinking streets, hopelessly drunk and in search of business. Once she would have met my blade and the streets would again have tasted blood. As I followed her, keeping to the shadows, I fantasized about tearing her open, steam coming from hot innards on cold cobblestones and finally silencing the whore's drunken ramblings. I followed her until the sky became grey with the pending dawn, before returning to my lodgings a frustrated and confused man.

Why did I ever stop?

The family which I swore to protect are turning against me. I'm sure Josephine is whispering to them when I am away, drawing them in to taking her side. She thinks I am a fool and she will pay for her betrayal when she and I are next alone. She thinks she knows violence but I have many tricks yet to show her. Perhaps it is time I established my authority on those who share in my household. After all is it not a man's right to control his family?

I tire of them all and am conscious that time is dwindling, and as I grow older my capabilities to do what must be done are waning.

I sense a change in me. The beast is stirring I do not care to stop it. Perhaps this is my destiny and my visit to London has re-ignited the desire to do what I do best.

I can hear muffled footsteps outside the door, and not for the first time wonder if they are watching and listening to me. Perhaps they are looking for this journal? I must be cautious. They think they know everything yet have no idea who I truly am and what I am capable of.

April 17th

The voices of the children reverberate inside my head, and for the first time, I wish them dead. Oliver is becoming more like his mother, weak and indecisive, and he is slowly but surely influencing Michael to behave the same way. Perhaps I would be doing them a service if I were to sever their arms and legs and toss the remains into the ocean. I feel little to no association with them. After all, they are someone else's children. I am their father only in name which is something I am increasingly grateful for. If any seed of mine were to grow into such weak-willed creatures I would have ended their pitiful existence long ago.

The bitch Josephine may have had an affair, thinking me too stupid to realise. Does she not think I see her as she walks around the house, desperate to avoid contact with me and whispering to the whore from the adjacent house? She thinks me a fool, and if she has taken a lover I intend to find out. Soon enough she will make a mistake that will justify the terrible retribution I have planned for her.

I yearn for the infamy which once surrounded me. I wonder if I should listen to the voice I have for a long time ignored.

May 26th

I have done a terrible thing.

Yesterday I was outside in the garden, enjoying the early morning sunshine before the heat became too oppressive. All was well until I headed back towards my refuge inside the house. I found the door to my study ajar and knowing I had closed it as I left, entered the room consumed by fury. The children were playing inside, the stupid bitch Josephine as always was not in control and allowing them to run unhindered around the house. Oliver was looking at the papers on my desk and had just set his hands upon this journal. I shudder to think what may have happened had I arrived any later. Lucy was with him looking through a pile of sketches based on some of my dreams, many of which were graphic in nature. I felt a blackness creep over me as the rage exploded. I grabbed Oliver and yanked him to the door, and unable to stop myself struck him in the face. The boy fell to the ground, his nose and lip bloodied. I then turned to Lucy and slapped her, holding nothing back. She too fell to the ground but unlike her brother she rounded on me, staring at me defiantly... she even smiled. I looked into the Childs' eyes and it was as if I were staring into a mirror. Perhaps there was some hope for one of these bastard children yet to be moulded into my image. Josephine heard the commotion, Oliver's wretched screams calling her from wherever she had been instead of attending to her duties.

The bitch was in front of me, pointing and screaming, telling me she would take the children and leave. It was here that my rage became complete. I grabbed her by the hair and took her upstairs as the children cried and screamed at my back, yet I cared little for their pleading. I'm not sure how long it took to serve the retribution for her carelessness, but when it was done we were both bloodied, and none of it was mine. I took her in every way, violating her as she begged for mercy. She scratched at my skin, but I have endured worse. I could not help myself and as our loveless coupling continued, I wondered if this was how insanity felt.

Oh, the giddy euphoria I felt as I closed my hands around her throat. I looked into her puffy, swollen eyes, past the blood and bruising, and ensured that she understood me. Her eyes were glassy, however, I made sure that the message was clear.

I told her I would kill her and the children before I would let them leave me alone again.

Why do they make me do such things?

If only they knew what a battle each day was for me just to live without returning to my work. My glorious work. I wonder how long a man can deny himself his calling. Great artists were meant to paint, great poets were born to recite, and great killers were made to kill.

Am I causing an injustice by not following what I was meant to do?

Is it better to go back to my work rather than cause this beast within me to manifest itself upon my family?

I will do as I always do and drink it away.

It is not a feeling I enjoy, however its end result means that for a time I can forget. I do not wish to write anymore. I am going to get some air and perhaps look in on the children and see if they are well following yesterday's incident. They have been avoiding me since it happened to which I can sympathize. The bitch Josephine I couldn't care any less for. She deserves all that she received and should think herself lucky that I didn't finish the job as she lay slumped on the floor. She hates me, yet doesn't realize that I showed her mercy in allowing her to live. If only she knew who I once was and that he was so close to regaining full control.

June 1st

I dreamed of my work last night. It was glorious in the way that dreams often are. All of my whores were merged into one glorious and bloody night. At the end I saw myself in the Kelly house, all five splayed out around me as I stood naked and blood-spattered as the house burned around us.

Am I going mad?

Certainly, I can feel the moorings of my mind beginning to loosen, and as each day passes I wonder more and more who I actually am. I have decided to write a letter to Abberline. I have been thinking about him a lot, and wish he were here. Of anyone perhaps he is the only one who understands who I am. I would like the two of us to sit over a meal and a good wine, and have a civil conversation about his hunt for me and my evasion of him.

Perhaps by now, he has another case to lead, another such as myself who is the subject of his attention. The thought of this fills me with not only incredible envy but also sadness. I have decided to write him a letter.

June 2nd

Letter to Abberline.

Dear Inspector Abberline.
I trust that you have not forgotten me. Although I have not graced Whitechapel with my work, you can

rest assured that I have not yet finished and will soon return to what I do best. I still want to do three in a single night if I can, and although out of practice I am sure you and I will soon become reacquainted.

I suspect that you may have doubts as to the authenticity of this letter, which after the slew of imitations is hardly a surprise. As proof of the legitimacy, how about this little snippet of information that only you and I would know.

You never found the Kelly woman's heart. Do not fret inspector, as I took it away with me wrapped in a red handkerchief and tied with string. It now sits in the drawer of this desk where I now write to you, a reminder of my great work.

I hope to see you soon inspector
Your friend
Jack The Ripper.

June 3rd

I have decided not to send the letter to Abberline. I fear it will stir up the hornets' nest when I am ill prepared for it to happen.

My urges have subsided somewhat but I do not know how long I can resist. I find that each year as August approaches which heralded the start of my work that I become more and more anxious and have to will myself not to act on the thoughts which will sometimes appear in my mind at the most inopportune times.

My intake of drink has become something of a concern, and I find that I am having to consume every day in order to maintain this farce of a life which I now lead. I am aware of the irony that I have become my father's son and worse still. The monstrous son of a lesser monster. I will write a memoir in the future and title it as such.

July 10th

This morning, I built a great bonfire in the garden and set ablaze all of my paintings. I no longer feel the joy of my work, or the desire to complete it. With the children away with Josephine, I have found time to reflect on my relationship with them. I do love them, however, my own misery is projecting itself onto them, and my all too short temper seems to manifest itself more easily in their presence.

It was different before when my temper and frustration was expended on the whores, leaving only the gentle and caring man to act as if he was a rational member of society. I can sense a rotten blackness within me, a dark pit of festering evil which has been there for as long as I can remember but no light. No good. What have I become? Have the whores turned me into this creature which even I do not understand?

I'm sure I know how to cure myself, and yet I cannot, as I know that if I begin my work again I will not be able to stop. As I write I am sitting by the picture window looking out over the ocean. I should feel grateful that wealth has afforded me such luxury, and yet I would give it away for just one more taste of my former life. The thrill of the act, the ripping of the flesh. Watching as the light of life fades from the dirty whore's eyes. I wonder what became of Lucy and that bastard who took her from me. Are they still together and in love? Do either of them still remember me?

September 2nd

I have purchased a new knife.

I visited a market by the coast when I happened upon a gentleman who had at his stall a huge array of blades. I paused to look and after a time drew a sharp intake of breath. My old knife, the one which helped me with my work sat before my very eyes. A sign from a higher power that I should not deny my work any longer! Not the exact same blade of course, as that one now lies at the bottom of the Thames, but it was near identical. I picked it up and felt a surge of power and excitement which has been absent for so long.

CHAPTER THIRTY FIVE

'Nothing to say, Hapgood? Have you finally learned the truth of the monster I am?'

'I have not yet reached the end, but must pause. I believed I had some sense as to the man you were. Now I am uncertain.'

'I warned you of the reality of who I was. *What* I am.'

Hapgood stood and paced. He was agitated and the physical and mental fatigue was making clear thought difficult. 'It is difficult to explain in words how reading this journal of yours makes me feel. It is as if the words are poison. They are affecting me more than I anticipated.'

'And this after reading a selection of pages from the briefest snapshot of my life. Try to imagine living with such a beast from birth.'

'I feel like an unwilling passenger in your mind, Miller as you make your inevitable stumble back to your murderous ways.'

Miller smiled.

'Something I said amuses you?'

'I mean no offence, Hapgood. I just enjoy your way with words. The drama you interject. The recommendations you have are well earned.'

'I apologise if my manner is sharp. I am quite exhausted by your story. Every time I believe I have heard the true extent of the horror I discover new depths of depravity. I will see no more this evening.'

'We had an agreement. I would tell all tonight and you would listen.'

Hapgood slammed his fist on the drinks cabinet. 'And I tell you I can take no more this evening.'

Miller stood, glaring at Hapgood. 'Do not make the error of forgetting with whom you speak.'

'Your threats are empty, Miller. You forget I've heard your story. I have seen how broken you are, coughing blood into your handkerchief. You were a monster once that is true. But as you stated yourself, you are a shell of that man.'

Rather than back down, Miller seemed to swell. He pushed his chest out and stood upright, a half smile on his thin lips, cold eyes glaring at Hapgood. 'Are you certain that is true? Are you sure that the weakness I have shown so far this evening is not designed to make my host feel more comfortable so he can complete his work without distraction? Are you certain, Hapgood that even now you are not conversing with the same monster who wrote those words which disturb you so?'

Hapgood hesitated, he was afraid, that was true, yet he had come too far to show it if he intended to control this situation. Miller went on, unmoved by Hapgood's protests.

'Did I not tell you, Hapgood, that he is a devious beast? That he will say anything to achieve his goal. He did it with the whores, whispering the words they wanted to hear before putting them to the blade and spilling their guts over the streets. Are you certain this broken old man does not carry one of his trusty knives with him in his pocket for this exact scenario?' Miller placed his hand on the breast pocket of his undercoat. 'How certain are you of my inability to revert to the monster you so fear? If you wish to see him in person, I can bring him out, however, I warn you. I will not be responsible for his actions. If you believe the written account of that beast is horrifying, it will pale next to witnessing that monster in the flesh. The decision rests with you, Hapgood. Do we continue our civil discussion or shall we see if you are right or wrong about my ability?'

Hapgood suspected Miller was a frail and broken old man, yet the risk was too great. Not for him as such, but for his wife and child. If he had learned anything since that long evening had begun, it was that he wanted them to have no part of this monster or his story. Hapgood shook his head and returned to his seat, sitting down hard. Miller continued to stare at him, his eyes full of life even if the vessel they were contained in was not.

'A wise choice, Hapgood. I have no desire to harm you this evening. I simply wish my story to be told. After this night, you and I shall never see each other again, of that, I can assure you. Now, however, you still have much reading ahead of you. Please, continue.'

Hapgood was going to respond then realised he had no idea what he would even say if he could. Instead, he tried to focus his exhausted mind and tired eyes on the journal. Taking a moment to compose himself, he dipped back into Miller's depraved mind.

November 3rd

I have taken ill. For the last few weeks I have found breathing difficult, and for the first time have not obsessed over my work. Today I feel a better despite my tiredness and even giddy with the medicines I have been given, I feel well enough to write.

I want to note an incident that occurred just a few days after my last entry into this journal.

I was walking through the market a few miles from here, my thoughts distracted by the humidity that made my clothes cling to my body in this ever-present hellish heat.

I was stopped by three young men who proceeded to produce a knife and demand money. The leader was confident, his eyes darting from side to side. Little did he know he had picked the worst possible person to stop. I looked him in the eye and smiled, pleased at the flicker of uncertainty I saw in response.

I asked him if he was familiar with the famous Whitechapel killer, Jack the Ripper.

The boy responded that he had, to which I pulled out my own knife, which was much bigger and sharper than his, then extended my hand to him and said I was pleased to meet him. He had opened his mouth to respond, and then I believe he saw something in me which told him I was telling the truth. He and his gang ran, leaving me disappointed that I did not get the chance to use my knife.

February 20th, 1892

I learned today that my old friend Abberline has retired. This has saddened me greatly, as I always imagined he and I would once again meet. I curse myself for not sending the letter which I had drafted to him. Perhaps it would have swayed his decision to leave the police force? Given him new motivation to solve the biggest mystery of them all.

Josephine asked me why my mood was so black and told me that the children were afraid of me. I struck her and told her she was not to trouble me anymore that day and that my business was my own.

Her reaction to this was most unexpected. She attempted to hit me with a vase, which inches closer would have struck me on the head. Within seconds I had her subdued. I dragged her to my study, and slammed her onto the desk, before grabbing my knife and holding it to her cheek. I believe she saw me then for what I truly am, and for a moment I was sure I was going to rip her there and then and leave her all over the desk. Memories of Mary Kelly flashed into my mind and I had to push them aside. Somehow I resisted, and tossed her to the ground, before telling her once again that she was my property to do as I want with, and if she or her bastard children were to utter another word without my permission I would cut out their tongues if it meant I would find peace.

April 7th

I wallow in misery. I am a stranger in my own home, and more so in my mind. I wonder if it is I who am in control, or if I am bound by the will of this dark evil that lives within me. I have begun to dream again, nightmarish visions of my work, ghoulish in their detail. They excite me and make me long for all that has passed. Often I wake in the night aroused by my dreams of blood and take my wife as she sleeps, violating her in whichever depraved manner comes to my mind. I am unable to reach sexual gratification without violence. It seems this was the root of the issue with Lucy all those years ago. I also believe I have become addicted to drink. I find myself constantly restocking my supply of whisky, and yet when morning comes I find only the empty bottle and a hazy recollection of the night before.

Gone is the lithe man I used to me, replaced by an overweight stranger.

Josephine continues to beg me to see a doctor. She says she is worried about me, but I know the truth. It is her and her children she is concerned for. Perhaps she is afraid that she will again ignite my temper and force me to do her harm. I swear I will do it. Next time I may cut off a finger if only to remind her to watch her tongue and keep her bastard children under control.

I cannot apportion all blame to her. She knows not of this beast which I harbour, nor the daily battle to keep it at bay. I wonder if I should tell her. Would she go to the police or would my rule of fear make her carry her share of my burden? It would be delightful to see it eat at her the same way it eats at me. The whore is weak-willed and would soon break from the burden. I am losing the strength to continue this fight and I fear for what I may do. I think I will go out tonight. Just to clear my head. Perhaps I will take my knife just for protection in what is a dangerous world.

April 9th

I offed a whore last night.

It was a messy, sloppy kill, the bitch screamed and clawed at me before she was silenced. I heard approaching footsteps and fled the scene before I could rip her open. I am disappointed with the outcome. My blade did not even reach to the bone.

I thought at the least this act would still the rage, and yet it seems to have stirred something deeper, and I find myself replaying the events, working out how next time to do the job properly.

Am I insane or am I just a man trying to find his rightful place in the world? I am of the belief that everyone has their calling, and mine is not husband, nor father nor artist. It is killer.

September 11th

It has been some time since I have felt the need to write in this macabre memoir, however, today felt like an excellent day to update on my progress. Life has made a sharp upturn for me, and for the first time, I feel hope. I no longer drink and have even shed all of the weight which I had gained.

My demon which has plagued me for so long lies dormant as I write this. Certainly, for the first time in recent memory, Josephine and I are again deeply in love. We do not talk about the dark times but look forward. The children also feel close to me, and as they grow up I cherish watching them learn the ways of the world as if they were my own.

Perhaps I can live a normal existence after all. Indeed, I at least owe it to myself and my family to try.

March 10th 1894

Josephine is with child, and I could not be happier. The thought of my first natural son or daughter making their way into the world is enough to push thoughts of my work away, and for the first time, I feel it is no longer the most important thing to me. I love all the children of course, but it is impossible to feel the same level of love for one who isn't of my own seed. This journal has been a constant during these last years, and although I could never bring myself to destroy it, I am afraid to read the earlier entries for fear of what I may see there from those darkest of times.

I think I will take a walk on the beach. The weather is beautiful, and I'm sure the children would like the chance to explore the sands.

November 13th

Josephine is having the child. The doctor is with her now in the upstairs bedroom and I am filled with giddy excitement. I wonder if I will have a son or a daughter. The children watch me through concerned eyes, and I smile and tell them all will be fine. They are growing so quickly that I feel as if I have missed so much. The boys are becoming fine young men. I should go to my wife and be with her as our new child enters the world.

November 14th

Last night, Josephine died whilst giving birth to my new born son, who also did not survive the ordeal. I feel as if the life has been expelled from my body also, and for the first time, I understand the sadness of death. I haven't told the children yet. They carry on in partial oblivion. They understand that something is amiss, however, they do not yet know the true implications of what has happened. They are in my care now, and I must do right by them. Keeping this journal is unhealthy, of that I am sure, however, it still gives me comfort to commit my thoughts to paper instead of keeping them within.

The future is uncertain, and I wonder if I will be a good parent. Time will tell, however, I must do what is right by them.

CHAPTER THIRTY SIX

'Mr Miller.... I am sorry for your loss.' Hapgood said as he looked up from the journal. Miller was motionless in the chair. It was clear he had been waiting for Hapgood to reach this part of the story. His cheeks were wet with tears.

'That was when I knew, Hapgood, that there was no hope for me. After first my mother, then Lucy and later Mary Kelly, I had always hoped there was a way to fight this beast. That night, as the doctor told me I had lost all that I loved, I came to understand that acceptance of my chosen path was the only way.'

'But the children, the other children I mean, they were still your responsibility.'

Miller nodded. 'Yes, they were. A responsibility I was far from prepared for. You will see for yourself soon enough what is to happen next. I have no desire to discuss it.'

'I understand, however-'

'Read on, Hapgood. Perhaps you will think again about offering your sympathy when you see the rest.'

November 18th

Josephine was buried today. As I sit here in the study, I can feel her presence still lingering and it makes my heart ache for her. Would she forgive me I wonder for my despicable deeds? By now she has met her God and knows the truth of who I am and of what I am responsible. She was a good woman who had deserved the love of a better man than I could ever be.

Alas, now it matters little and I begin to wonder how I will fill the void left by her sudden demise. The obvious answer is one which I cannot entertain.

The circumstances have changed in that I now have a responsibility to Michael, Oliver and Lucy. For now, I will set aside this journal and turn my energies towards taking care of them.

December 31st, 1900

The children have been taken from me. Despite my efforts, I failed to give them sufficient love and care, and the violence which once manifested itself on my wife instead found its way to them. I am glad they are gone for both their sake and mine. They are not mine and deserve better than to live in this place with a monster like me. This house feels so large and empty for one person alone. I walk its rooms at night, like a ghastly spectre and ask myself why I am left to suffer in solitude. Is this a sign? Perhaps God wants to me to continue with my work and has removed all distractions. I feel as old and worn as this journal, the glue which holds the pages of my mind in place is beginning to crack and fail.

I have killed only twice more since my last entry. The first was an old whore who reminded me of Nichols, her I ripped on the beach and pushed her filthy body out to sea.

The second was a young boy, a first for me. It was the first anniversary of Josephine's death, and I was delirious with grief and the worse for alcohol.

He was perhaps eight or nine years old, and before I realised what had happened I had cut off his arms, legs and head and tossed them into the sea. I was chilled by the calm and ease with which I accomplished the work. It was as if I had never stopped.

I wept later that evening and considered ending my existence.

I am rarely able to sleep of late, which is why I have again taken to writing in this journal. The old habit that began in Whitechapel has stayed with me during these years and it helps to write my true feelings without fear of discovery.

My days are spent in my study, where I now sleep, sometimes drinking and at other times lost in thought. On an evening I cannot bear to be in the house. It has become a cold and desolate place and I fear I can hear ghosts of the past walking its rooms. On more than one occasion I am certain I have seen Josephine, clad in white as she walks the stairways and she calls out for her children

In my solitude, I have taken to coaxing the voice long forgotten from the inner reaches of my mind so that I am not alone. I need its comfort, its companionship and its wisdom.

February 16th, 1901

I am going back to London to continue my great work. There is nothing to keep me here now, and I long for the chill weather of England. I have a few affairs to attend to here in Florida, not least of which is selling the house. It has fallen into disrepair, and I have had neither the inclination nor enthusiasm to attend to it. It has become a tomb, the prison cell I had been so desperate to escape when I fled from Whitechapel. I cannot stay here anymore.

The thought of returning home excites me. Before I sell the house, I am going to destroy any evidence that links me to my identity. I am also undecided on if I should leave this journal behind in the hope that someday it will be found and the truth of my identity will be discovered. Perhaps then I will get the deserved recognition for my work.

I long for the start of my work and the warmth of their fresh blood on my cold hands. I wonder in Abberline's absence who will be my new nemesis?

It is too much to hope that he might see fit to come from retirement and resume his search for me? I know that it must pain him to have never caught me. How will he react to my return when he reads his morning newspaper?

I am growing anxious, and find myself pacing, unable to sleep as night turns to day. The time is near and in just a few short weeks I will begin my great work once more.

June 1901

Returning to the capital is akin to returning to a love long forgotten. I have taken lodgings in the heart of Whitechapel. I was but a stone's throw away from where my old work took place and the thrill is more than I could ever hope to illustrate with words. The streets still crawl with the filthy vermin, and as before I plan to begin in September. I long for the cold of night and the frenzy that will be caused when Jack returns to plague the whores of London.

July 1901

I have walked the streets of Whitechapel to familiarise myself once more with its winding streets. Little had changed. Whores and vermin on every corner. I lost count of the number of times I was propositioned by the filthy cunts. It was fortunate for them I did not have my knife otherwise

I would have done them there and then no matter the consequences.

August 31st

The air holds a chill tonight which excites me as September draws closer. I feel healthy and strong, and for the first time in many a year, my mind is clear. The inner voice which has plagued me for so long now comforts me, and we are both ready to work together as one in order to continue my great work.

The feel of the blade on flesh will be akin to the tender embrace of a love long lost.

Today is the anniversary of the day I did one of the whores. The children's faces are hard for me to recollect, yet the events of that night still live in my mind with absolute clarity. My anxiety to continue my work is great, and I must choose when I will start.

The tenth of the month is an option and will afford me the extra few days which I need in order to sharpen my blade. I will take additional lodgings deep within the heart of Whitechapel. Somewhere secluded and private will not be hard to find amid such squalor.

September 7th
I have decided that the tenth is the day.

September 11th

I missed out on the deed last night. I had chosen the bitch and was about to strike when I was disturbed and was forced to leave her alive without even cutting her. I am angry to have it snatched away so cruelly. I am growing old, and time is beginning to be something I am acutely aware of as the years pass me by. I miss my wife, my beautiful Josephine. I know now I was cruel to her, and despite this, she always stood beside me and my demons.

How I long for her to be here now and comfort me.

September 14th

It is done. The bitch bled better than I could have ever hoped, and even as she lay in the filth with her stomach ripped open wide, still, she would not die!

It was wonderful, I looked into her eyes as I pulled it out, coil after coil of it and showed it to her. I took some of it with me and fed it to a stray street dog. I feel like a twenty-year-old man again and await word of my work in the newspapers.

September 16th

It seems a ripped whore is no longer a newsworthy item. I checked the papers for news of my great deed, but it appears I have truly been forgotten and in this world, dead whores are aplenty. Still, it is only because they do not know it was I who was responsible. They do not know the Ripper they so fear is back to work. It matters not. Tonight, I shall go out again and do another, and this time I will leave them in no doubt that I have returned to haunt them. They WILL fear me. They WILL remember my name.

September 16*th*

It is impossible. How could the whore so easily wrestle my knife from me? The wound in my side is deep and requires stitches, but I cannot visit a hospital. The bitch kicked and fought and used my own knife against me. The strength I felt inside would not manifest within my physical body. I ran from her, blood pooling between my fingers as he held onto my side, the whore waving my knife at me as I fled into the shadows. I could hear her cackling and threatening to finish me.

Something has changed.

When I was last here the bitch would have been dispatched with ease, and yet here she was my equal and I am worse for injuries. When I returned to my lodgings the pain in my chest was stronger even than that of the knife wound in my side.

Damn this body of mine!

I must have this wound tended to. I have dressed it as best I can but it still bleeds and I feel weak.

September 17*th*

I am fixed. I paid a man who claimed to be a doctor to stitch my wound. His work was shoddy, his surgery filthy, yet he did what I asked. Even though he was paid to ask no questions, I gave him a reason for my injuries, feeding him the same story I gave some years ago that I had been mugged by a street gang. The doctor, several years my junior, said the streets were dangerous and someone of my age should consider staying indoors after dark. How I wanted to cut him as he said it, but I knew I was too weak and he would be more than a match for me physically. I fled here to this hovel where I stay, confused and frustrated.

I looked in the mirror to observe myself as the surgeon did, and saw the truth in his words. I feel like a young man but my appearance was anything but. The years have been unkind and I look every bit the weak old fool the whore managed to fight off so easily. For the first time, I have doubts that I am able to complete my work. The idea that I will be denied it frightens me. Surely the whore who fought me so viciously is an isolated incident. I will make my grand return.

September 24th.

My injury is healed but I cannot bear to look at the wound. It screams failure and reminds me I am a weaker man than I once was. I ask the demon inside me for its reassurance yet it remains silent. It is awaiting blood and will not respond until it receives it.

Very well. Tonight we shall try again.

I have purchased a new knife to replace the one the whore took from me. Tonight the one I rip will pay the price for the actions of her fellow whore.

September 29th

This will be the final entry I make before I tie rocks to my feet and jump into the Thames.

I realise now that it is too late. I have wasted too much time and the opportunity to do as I once did is something my ageing body is no longer capable. Three consecutive nights now I have set out to attempt my work and three nights have ended in failure of the most spectacular variety.

The first was much like the previous whore, only this time I managed to keep my knife. She fought and screamed, kicked and scratched until aid came. I was fortunate to escape without being caught.

The second was worse still. I coaxed her into the dark, ready to do my work when she took a knife to me and stole my money. I will admit in these pages that I was afraid of her, and as she took everything I had, blade pressed to my cheek I wished she would have cut my throat and be done with it. The ultimate embarrassment, robbed by a stinking filthy whore.

The last was the worst of them all. Driven by frustration and anger at my failure, I was aggressive and found a dark corner in which to do my work, however, as my hands closed around her throat she pushed me off and laughed at me. I could do nothing but stand there and stare at her as she cackled in the gloom. I ran, then. Winding through dark alleyways and past public houses full of rowdy patrons. I did not stop until the pain in my chest returned and breathing became next to impossible. It was then, as I stood in the shadow of the church that I knew it was over. There would be no grand return. No more striking fear into the whores of Whitechapel. My body had failed me, and now there is nothing left for me but the blessed silence of death. I have destroyed everything I ever loved in this world and in turn the world has destroyed me. Soon enough it will end. Tomorrow I will visit whatever lies beyond head on. Perhaps then I will find my peace.

CHAPTER THIRTY SEVEN

'That's the final entry.' Hapgood said, closing the journal. Miller was staring into the fire. Hapgood waited for his guest to speak, but Miller held his silence.

'Mr Miller?'

'What more is there to say? The story is told. You have read to its conclusion.'

Hapgood shuffled, his mind ablaze with thoughts and ideas, questions he was reluctant to leave unanswered. 'But... there is much still I do not understand.'

'Have you not learned enough?' Miller snapped.

'My intention is not to hound you but to ensure I have all the information required to tell your story.

'I am tired, Hapgood as I am sure you are also. What more is there that you wish to know?'

'The ending. You talked of death. Leaping into the Thames with rocks tied to your feet. That was seven years ago. I would like to know what has happened since that last entry and now. More specifically, why you changed your mind.'

Miller stood and walked to the window, his back to Hapgood. 'Daylight is coming. This has indeed been a long evening. As to your question, I had every intention of ending my life. I was determined and spent the rest of that evening drinking as much alcohol as I could. I was too afraid to sleep, you see. Every time I closed my eyes I would see one of them. The whores. My mother. Lucy. Josephine. Their spirits haunted my existence.'

He turned to face Hapgood, folding his hands in front of him. 'The only one who did not want my pitiful life to end was the bastard thing that lives inside me. It was still thirsty for blood and it would not allow me to end my existence.'

'And did you try to resist?'

'Of course, I did, but it was much stronger than I was and would not allow it. I came close to achieving my wish a few weeks later. I drank the monster to its pit and made it there to the bridge, rocks tied to my feet, the black waters of the Thames which would signal freedom swirling beneath me. I wanted to let go, Hapgood. I wanted it more than perhaps anything else I have ever desired, and yet it would not allow me to do so no matter how much I begged. As broken as I was, it was still thirsty for blood.'

'How then, have you managed during these intervening years without your work? Surely if this…inner you was so influential, it would be impossible to resist.'

Miller smiled but it was without humour, and the expression quickly melted away. 'Ahh yes, and with that question, we come back to the start. My darkest days, as it were.'

'I don't understand.'

Miller walked to the drinks cabinet and poured himself another drink. He did not ask Hapgood, who watched as Miller drained the glass then set it back on the cabinet. 'It was no longer possible to do my work on the whores, but the beast still desired blood, so we reverted back to childhood habits. At least they were still in our power to control.'

'Animals?'

Miller nodded. 'Oh yes, I'm sure there are countless animal victims of the once famous Whitechapel Ripper scattered around these filthy streets. Stray dogs and cats mostly as the even the rats were now too fast for me to capture.' Miller grimaced and shook his head. 'And that is how I have existed since, killing animals and wishing they were whores as year on year my body becomes weaker and slips ever closer to death. An uninspiring end to my legend, do you not agree?'

Hapgood said nothing. Miller went on, pouring another drink.

'You see the irony of the situation, Hapgood? They speak of me today as a thing of legend, a supernatural being who had the ability to do his work without fear of reprimand by the authorities before disappearing into the darkness, leaving behind a mystery like no other.' Miller drained his glass again, then tossed it on the cabinet.

'Please, Mr Miller, I think perhaps that is enough drink for now.'

Miller ignored him, continuing on as his voice became ever more slurred. 'The truth is I was here the whole time in Whitechapel, unable to leave because I had nowhere to go, a lonely old man too broken to live and not allowed to die as he spent his days and nights killing animals to sate some desire that he knows would never again be fully satisfied. I am pleased to say that I can finally sense death and it is close. I cannot wait for it to take me. There is no treatment for my illness, Hapgood. My insides continue to rot and with each day brings more and more intense pain.'

Miller pointed at Hapgood, swaying on unsteady legs. 'I know what you are thinking. I can see it in your eyes. You are easy to read. You think I deserve the pain, the agony of a slow death, a life of suffering amid the subjects of my work and yet physically incapable of acting on the ideas which present themselves to my mind.'

Hapgood glanced to the door, the fear he had forgotten over the last hours coming back in an instant. 'Please remain calm, Mr Miller. I am here to listen to and log your story. Nothing more. My own feelings bear no influence on our meeting this evening.'

Miller sneered. 'Yet you feel it all the same.' He crossed the room to Hapgood's desk, leaning on it palms first, glaring at Hapgood. 'You are no different to everyone else. You live within the boundaries of the law, you have a nice home, a family. A life. Those are the things I wanted, yet was born with a demon, a blood hungry parasite. I am a victim.'

The comment was too much for Hapgood. He had heard and read enough to know the truth. 'You are no victim. You preyed on the weak, the vulnerable. You have admitted as much yourself.'

Miller grinned. 'Look at you. No longer afraid now you know how the story ends. Do you know who I am?'

Hapgood stood, staring Miller in the eye from across the table, his own anger at Miller claiming he was a victim making him forget the fear. 'I know who you *were*. Now I see a broken old man who is unwilling to take responsibility for the horrific things he did as he desperately clings to a life in the past.'

Miller grimaced. 'You will show me the respect I deserve.'

'You deserve no respect, Miller. You deserve to be held accountable for your crimes. Perhaps I am guilty of listening to this tale for too long. I should have notified the authorities upon your arrival and had them come and take you away. Those poor women you savaged deserve justice for the brutality you reigned upon them whe-'

Miller moved fast. A flick of the wrist. Hapgood was unsure what had happened at first until he heard the steady dripping. He looked at his desk and saw it was splattered with blood. His once white shirt was red across the belly where Miller had slashed him. Hapgood sat down hard in his chair, feeling his innards start to poke out of the wound. He could see the knife now. Miller had it clutched in his right hand. Hapgood had no clue where he had got it from and assumed he must have had it with him all along just as he had alluded to earlier in the evening. A second of silence fell over the room which Miller broke. He was staring at Hapgood, watching the blood ooze from his stomach.

'Did I not warn you? I told you not to forget who I am. True enough, I can no longer rip whores, but you….I had gained your trust. Your guard was down. One cut is all it takes if it is deep enough.'

Hapgood was clutching his stomach, trying to hold the contents in. 'Help. I need help…' he murmured.

'I would recommend you do not stand, Hapgood. I have cut across your lower abdomen. Who knows what will fall out?'

'You…you said you ….wouldn't hurt me. You said I would live.'

'Yes, I did. But did I not also tell you that this thing inside me will say anything to get what it wants?'

'You came to me…you wanted me to tell your story…'

Miller nodded and picked up his journal. 'May I borrow your pen?'

Hapgood was bleeding from the mouth now. He was gasping and didn't respond.

'There is time for one last entry. A final footnote in the story.'

Miller opened the journal to the final entry. 'You seem preoccupied, Hapgood so I will dictate to you as I write. Perhaps then you will truly understand the meaning of tonight.'

Hapgood tried to answer but could only groan. He shifted position and a wet coil of intestine spilt out between his fingers. Miller half smiled then turned his attention to the journal and began to write, reading his words out loud as he penned them.

'And so, we come to this. The end. The demon inside is as tired as I am and we both long for peace. The Biographer, Hapgood who came so highly recommended was as good as the reputation he had built. He has logged everything and despite earlier this evening stating that he was no priest and would not hear my confession that is exactly what he has done. It was his task. A way for me to ensure at least one person knew who I was and heard of my great work. Sadly, this story can never leave this house. How could I sully my legend by allowing the world to know the great Ripper ended his days killing cats and dogs in the squalor of his filthy Whitechapel home? No, my demon and I are in agreement. Our story has been told to Hapgood and he, like us, will take it to his grave.' Miller stopped writing and glanced up at Hapgood, who was motionless, eyes blank and staring across the room. Miller continued on, still dictating to the room. 'As I write this he has already slipped away, gone to whatever comes after. Despite for many years seeing our great work as a failure, it seems in the intervening years my legend has grown and will endure for centuries long after my broken body is dust. A fitting end, then to a great story, and now with conscience clear thanks to Hapgood I can live out my remaining days in relative peace without the burden of the years weighing on me. This then is the end of the story. Hapgood knew me as Mr Miller, and for the purpose of telling my story that was necessary.

If by some chance I had failed in my plan tonight, I could not allow Hapgood to know my true identity, however now I shall sign off in the name I was given, the name people will try to discover for hundreds of years to come, the identity of the great Whitechapel killer before this journal is destroyed along with Hapgood's notes.

With this then, I say farewell. The story is at last, over. I shall once again become a ghost and in my stead, I shall leave my legend, my legacy, my great work. History will come to remember me by the name they gave me, and in that respect it is clear the work I set out to complete is, at last, done. My physical body will die but I shall live on forever.

My name is ▬▬▬▬ ▬▬▬▬▬▬ and I was Jack the Ripper.'

EPILOGUE

The inferno reached high into the early morning sky, the Mountford Street home completely gutted as the fire raged on. A crowd had gathered outside the home of the Hapgood family and looked on powerless as the flames continued to eat the building to the brickwork. The crowd speculated and questioned if the family were home. Some murmured that the wife and children were away but the husband, Charles was home.

'He was home,' one man snapped.

The other onlookers glanced at him as he stood and watched the flames.

'How do you know?' Someone else asked.

Abberline looked at him, the sharpness in the former detective's eyes having lost none of their intensity with retirement. 'Because Charles is a friend of mine. He had invited me here today to discuss my memoirs. I used to be a police inspector.'

'I hope he wasn't at home,' the man said, showing more respect to the retired inspector.

'At this hour so early in the morning it is likely he was,' Abberline said. He stared at the house, the gut feeling instinct of a police officer still as strong as ever. There was no chance anybody could have survived such an inferno.

'You don't think somebody would have done this deliberately, do you?'

Abberline glanced at the man who had fallen into line beside him. He didn't address the inspector directly, but stared at the fire, the flames seeming to dance in his eyes. A pang of something - recognition, perhaps- gnawed in Abberline's gut, but he could not place where he knew the man from.

'I can't think of anyone who would wish to harm them.' The inspector muttered as he stared at the fire.

'No, I agree. Charles was a gentleman, of that there is no doubt, and yet death waits for no man. It comes when it desires and we are powerless to stop it.'

Abberline glanced at him again, still searching through the vault of hundreds of people he had met over the years to put a name to the face. 'You speak as if you know for sure he's already dead.'

The man half smiled, a cruel twist of the lips. 'Just an assumption based on the intensity of the flame. Nothing more.'

Abberline looked at the man again, frustrated at his inability to recall. 'Do you know something about this fire?'

The man looked at the inspector, his expression neutral. 'Of course not. Surely you don't think I am capable of such a terrible thing. What you are looking for is a monster, and I am clearly not that.'

Another surge of recollection erupted in Abberline at those words. He had heard them before. It sounded like something he might say. A collective gasp from the crowd distracted him as the sagging roof of the house collapsed inward, sending a fresh plume of smoke and flame into the ever lightening sky. Abberline glanced back to speak to the man to ask him his name, but he was gone. Abberline pushed through the growing crowd to find him again, the nagging in his gut not going away. He pushed out of the crowd, looking both ways up and down the street, but the man had gone, already lost in the maze of alleys and side streets.

www.ingramcontent.com/pod-product-compliance
Lightning Source LLC
LaVergne TN
LVHW011927070526
838202LV00054B/4520